17. F V34460

FREEDOM FOR
MR MILDEW
AND
NIGEL SOMEONE

Clive Murphy

FREEDOM FOR
MR MILDEW
AND
NIGEL SOMEONE

LONDON : DENNIS DOBSON

To my Mother

and

Maureen MacDonnell

The extract from the song 'Delilah', written by Les Reed and Barry Mason, is reproduced by kind permission of Donna Music Ltd.

The extract from the song 'Congratulations', written by Bill Martin and Phil Coulter, is reproduced by kind permission of The Peter Maurice Music Company Ltd.

The extracts from *The Jungle Book, Just So Stories*, 'The Glory of the Garden' and 'The Ballad of East and West' by Rudyard Kipling are reproduced by kind permission of Mrs George Bambridge and The Macmillan Company of London and Basingstoke.

First published in Great Britain 1975 by
Dobson Books Ltd, 80 Kensington Church Street, London, W8

Printed in Great Britain by
Bristol Typesetting Co, Ltd,
Barton Manor, St Philips, Bristol

ISBN 0 234 77278 6

Being free isn't doing what other people
like to do; it's doing what *you* like
to do.

H.R.H. The Prince of Wales
in *The Observer* 9th June 1974

FREEDOM FOR MR MILDEW
For Kenneth MacGowan

I

Monday/Tuesday, 15th/16th April, 1968

Exile is my privilege. There isn't room in England for a Toby
Mildew. To offer a Girl Guide shelter for the night is here re-
garded as more culpable than treason. Yet were I, in this carriage, to raise my glass and cry 'To the Devil with Her Majesty!'
a hand-clap and 'Hear! Hear!' would be my only penalty.

The students chant that they will overcome. They believe that
by rolling marbles under horses' hooves they will dismount the
forces of oppression. Rather will the Ghost Squads effect their
walkie-talkie raids and house arrests more vigorously. Boos to
geese will provoke the Commissioner.

In Besançon, no rabble-rousing will disturb the mood of my
researches, and I can rest awhile from the baiting of our Official
Conscience. At liberty to recover from my prison sentence and
enjoy rights forfeited at home, I shall once again feel com-
petent to write my best and to serve my Editor without constraint.

To render responsible service, d'être utile à quelqu'un, à
quelqu'une, has always been my endeavour. 'Fetch me my gloves,
mon bijou!' 'Run get me my Gamblers' Compendium!' 'Go see
if there are any gâteaux secs in the pantry!' 'Where's my eau de
cologne?' Such joy it gave me rummaging and searching! I
would return triumphant for Mother's reward of a bon-bon or a
kiss.

Maman was Huguenot, so Sundays we went to church. I
mention it to remind myself that I am not an ungodly man. I
have retained since childhood a healthy respect for the unknown.
Readings from the lectern influenced me for good.

As did Grand-maman. Each summer, while Father remained
at home in Oxfordshire and Mother gambled on the Côte d'Azur,

A*   9

I served her happily in Malaucène. To me she was as steadfast as Mont Ventoux on whose billowy slopes her small house rested. At cock-crow I would creep to join her in her kitchen, proud to turn the pages of her cookery book as, preparing for the day ahead, she pottered amid scents of savory, nutmeg, coriander and thyme. I never broke the magic of her ritual with speech till long after the shivering phantom of the night Mistral had vanished and it was glorious snail-hunting, poppy-picking morning.

When, holding a letter in her hand, my mother told me she had gone to paradise, a tear trickled down my left cheek. In that tear was my very essence. I have never visited Provence since, without recalling her gargoyle tulips planted on the sills in buckets and tin-cans, her lavender bags, the trellis for her bower of roses, the elastoplast labels on her kitchen jars. When in my writings, I decry the sentimentalism of Maurice Barrès; when I refuse to drink Châteauneuf du Pape; when I denounce the touristic exploitation of Avignon and Vaison-la-Romaine, it is in self-defence against the desolation of her dying. She was as much a mother to me as my own. She read me 'Mother Goose' and 'Les Enfants et les Bêtes'. More than anyone, more than my tutors, she taught me how to spell.

I had no reason to respect my mother, any more than did my father who stayed making furniture in his workshop at almost every hour of every season, deliberately blind-eyed to her self-indulgence. It became my task to pamper her throughout the years, brushing her hair from gold to grey, raking and tugging at her tresses to words of endearment and to little groans. That, indeed, was service.

The tutors she chose for me always left. With each it was the same :

'You *will* try to help him, mon petit ?'

'Why should I ?'

'I shall speak to your father about sending you to school !'

'Oh, very well.'

I helped them, Monsieur This and Monsieur That. 'Qu' est-ce que c'est que ceci?' one of them once asked, putting a hand upon my private parts. 'It's nothing to do with you', I replied. I was only ten, and my sang-froid must have unnerved him for he flushed crimson. His was the first threat of sexual intimacy I had ex-

10

perienced, except for maman squeezing a sponge over me when I was in the bath. Strange how the mildest of episodes can amount to an eating of the fruit.

Afternoon tea was the only meal at which the family met together. With what care maman infused verbena for the benefit of Father and me, but especially me! With what expectancy she produced the petits fours she spent her Tuesdays baking! Yet the silences were overwhelming. I felt her longing for my affection waft around the room. She scrutinized me as I ate each mouthful, sipped each drop. Even the crumbs, the moisture on my lips, were objects of concern. 'Use your napkin, chéri.'

Father ate without a murmur. Once I heard him say, 'Leave the boy alone!' My heart pounded at this birth of interest, something to spare me from the merciless focus of maman's attention. I longed to tell him, 'It's you I need! It's you I need!' But I guarded my secret and he remained aloof. Always I mentioned his name in bedtime prayers. Twice I did some simple carpentry at his request. Though later our maid, beloved Annie, became the object of my adolescent yearnings, I served him as faithfully as I knew how, until a German bomb reduced my home to rubble and deprived me both of parents and of her.

Dover Marine. The first stride towards a fresh beginning successfully completed. Besançon one stage nearer; Besançon where, beyond ridicule, beyond the prying good-will of well-wishers, I shall nourish my misinterpreted affections. There I shall thrive again. The plant that was temporarily relegated to darkness shall flower in sunlight.

The carriage is shunted into the boat's belly. The fibres of my frustrated body thrill at the prospect of deliverance. Haha! The Henchmen of the Law cannot reach me here! I'll lock the door and hide till called at eight. Then, in sweet France, where Napoleon saved the people from the justice of the courts, I shall again roam free. But come! Where's my courage? Why not a last defiant glance at my accusers and the country that tormented me?

I ring for the attendant.

'Which staircase to the shop?'

'Monsieur can avoid the crowds by taking the second door.'

Avoid the riff-raff. He, too, has soul.

'A pound for you.'

'Monsieur is too kind.'

But would he say it did he know how often I surrender to my nature and fasten young and febrile bodies to my side in friendship? I curse the Puritans who restrain me from these tender skills. I pity the harshly indoctrinated schoolgirls who have not met a respectful Toby Mildew before they flaunt themselves as students on the streets.

Imprisoned for Indecent Assault.

Fiddlesticks! Imprisoned for integrity more like!

I have made my purchases. A bottle of scent may suit some pretty lass. Dover Castle has faded, the castle over which the bomber sped that sent my parents and my lover to their doom. A lout beside me in the bar smokes Woodbines. Beyond the window, in the rectangle of black between green curtains, a golden moon slides up and down the sky.

'I always get a kick out of this.'

It's the lout smoking Woodbines. He's addressing himself to me.

'Out of what?' I feign incomprehension.

'Crossing the Channel.'

'For me not an unusual occurrence.'

'For me it's ever so rare.'

'You must re-arrange your life.'

'Easier said than done!'

'I have always found it easier to do than say!' I exaggerate to raise us from the marshes.

'You're a card!'

He stretches out a gnarled hand.

'Your Easter holidays?' I inquire.

'You must be joking!'

I'm intrigued, despite his limitations.

'How long are you spending in France?'

'Only a couple of days. Have to get back then to collect my strike pay.'

'Amoralist!'

'You only live once. "I love Paris . . ."'

He starts to sing the common tune.

'So you're Paris bound?'

'Yes. And you?'

'Besançon.'

'Never 'eard of it.'

'More's the pity.'

'Tell me about it.'

I protect myself against his ignorance:

'To what purpose?'

'I might give it a try if you persuaded me.'

'The capital of the Franche-Comté. Were you to consult the bibliographies, you would discover it possesses a by no means negligible political and military history.'

'No ooh-la-la?'

'Not my line, I'm afraid.'

I rise to go.

'Hey hey! No offence intended.'

Standing by my chair, I apologize for my abruptness:

'I am rather out of sorts.'

'Sit yourself down then, mate, and I'll order you a can of beer!'

Involuntarily I pull a face.

He is not deterred:

'Have something else then!'

'A glass of water.'

We cross to the counter.

'Water. Make it a double. And, for me, another pint of the jolly old brew . . .'

He banters with the barman. They are two of a kind.

'My name's Jeff. What's yours?'

'Mildew. Tobias Mildew.'

I had planned to stay anonymous.

'Pleased to meet you. Well, cheerio, Mr Mildew. Down the hatch! This is what I like about a spree!'

Back on my bunk I snatch at sleep but it evades me. I switch off the light. I switch it on. I raise the blind, forgetting there's no view save the girders of the ferry's hold. I am a coiled spring. I am sensitive and vibrant. Whose are the hands that will unwind me? Must the nights contain no more than punishment?

Fitful sleep. A tremor. Then silence, followed by much shouting. I open the door. The blinds of the corridor windows have

13

been drawn. I hurry to the end of the last carriage, deploring the possibility of some fresh disaster which will rob me of rejuvenation.

Snores filter from the berths. Sailors, mechanics in blue overalls, customs officers, agents de police, bustle and shake hands outside. A grey bridge is lowered in the twilight—my bridge to fredeom, to safety, to reversal of fortunes on foreign soil. O ripening moment! At a hundred paces, where Liberty dwells, there is my adopted country!

'S'il vous plaît, Monsieur.'

A streak of terror lances me from head to toe.

A representative of the Law menaces in cape and képi. My bid for freedom has been flouted. A section of some Act of Parliament has undone me as before. At the brink, at the very frontier of happiness, my efflorescence has again been thwarted.

'Vos bagages, Monsieur.'

'Heaven forfend us! At such an hour! Yours a civilized country? I've filled in the forms. I've purchased no more than the permitted quotas . . .'

My voice rattles on in hysterical relief as he accompanies me to my luggage.

He apologizes for disturbing me.

'Not at all, Monsieur,' I reassure him. 'Thank *you*'. 'Goodnight, Monsieur, goodnight!'

Tremblingly I hoist my belongings to the rack, then return to my post of observation.

The train waits in its opened cage, tense as a tethered beast about to break its chains and leap into the vast, murky questionmark of a preferable unknown. In the distance, the headlights of a low and noiseless motorcar briefly illuminate the hulk of a laden goods-van.

Now a lantern swings, and slowly, second by slow second, the hand that holds it, the body to which that hand belongs, emerge from obscurity, as does a moving inky blur behind it—the engine which is to lead us to our pastures new.

First the carriages on tracks parallel with mine are linked and brought away. O happy ones to be so preferred! Then the receding mass reverses. A twin oblong softly approaches to meet mine. I step backwards, press against the wall to withstand the jolt of union. Two youths leap to secure the couplings. Fair

France, while slumbering, receives me. To her I commit my future happiness.

Stretched on my bunk, I watch the dawn among the derricks of Dunkerque, and murmur to myself the stanza from Coleridge's immortal ode:

> Thou rising Sun! thou blue rejoicing Sky!
> Yea, everything that is and will be free!
> Bear witness for me, wheresoe'er ye be,
> With what deep worship I have still adored
> The spirit of divinest Liberty.

Crisp as salad, lusty as a mountain stag without a cerebral nuage, I see the tracts of brown and green flick by. I've shed the months of misery with reptilian finesse.

Meticulous rows of poplar impart to my exuberance security and logic. I scoop more confiture onto my roll, and eat with satisfaction. A peasant at my table slops his coffee from cup to cup to cool it. I do not complain. Like Jeff, he's something ordinary I must learn to suffer. A piggy grunting in a beret; a country hick—he'll know, as I do, what this mistletoe, huge nests of it near Creil, is growing on. I speak:

'Excuse me, Monsieur. What are these trees the mistletoe has chosen?'

'Mistletoe trees.'

'Are they not birch?'

'No, mistletoe trees.'

To prevent me probing his ignorance further, he hands me a copy of L'Aurore.

I shake with laughter as I accept it. I've never felt so gay.

85 DEAD, 713 WOUNDED on the Easter Roads.

I confirm with my reflection in the pane that I'm very much alive.

Miss Bette Davis, I read on, regrets her marriages. The words lend melody to my bachelordom.

I bask in inner pleasures. A maiden sits two tables from me. I play with myself beneath the cloth. A warmth pervades my being, binds me to her in an ecstasy of sensual contentment. The simplest movements of the hand conjure mind and body into

15

spiralling convolutions. Oh yes, my dear! Your cheeks suffuse my own with the blushing tenderness of a mutual understanding. Toby Mildew, unlike the present generation of novice Romeos, has no need of stimulants to cause or to prolong his bliss. These fingers, rhythmically attuned, transform the meanest dining-car into a chariot which rides the outer limits of the stratosphere . . .

I return to my writing. I dare not be too reckless till arrival at my destination, till my enterprise has properly begun.

Outside the Gare du Nord, I can't be bothered queuing for a taxi. I tell the porter to take my bags to a voiture de luxe.

'Gare de Lyon. And please stop somewhere I can buy a collar stud.'

We park at a men's outfitter's in the shadow of the Bastille column.

'You'll find your collar stud in there. Be quick. Traffic regulations . . .'

'Here too! Don't speak to me of regulations. In England . . .'

'Monsieur is not French!'

I try to explain from the pavement. He interrupts me.

'Monsieur must not be too long.'

Impertinence!

I consider losing my temper, but refrain. Why squander sensibility on yet another philistine? Three hours and I'll be out of Paris. I must not allow it to take too great a toll on my emotional resources.

I register my luggage so as to wander the station and its environs unimpeded. The clerk is sniggering. My panama amuses him. I hear the word 'chapeau' as I walk away. My fault again. I shouldn't fraternize. To restore my good temper I suggest the body of a girl with a few deft penstrokes on the wall of a WC. Before the owner of approaching feet is able to detect me, I am standing nonchalantly at my stall.

I cross the road.

The floor of the Café Européen is an ashtray. I order a coffee—large and black. A cockade of hair projects from the waiter's forehead as though he were a circus horse. There's a woman at the table opposite squeezing a man's face for blackheads. She sighs rapturously as each one oozily emerges. He is hers to be kept repaired, unblemished, like a kitchen dresser.

16

The sky is grey. The plane trees are dusty. I return to the station.

Whores are scanning the arcade for custom.

'Tu désires quelque chose?'

How I despise the unsolicited 'tu'!

I delay at the photomaton, transfixed by rituals displayed before submission to the camera's lens—the nervous titillations, the pulling and plucking at garments by women coyly waiting for their turn.

At last I am alone. I hasten to be photographed myself—not out of vanity, but because Besançon University, whose canteen and library are to be at my disposition, requires that I commit my countenance in triplicate to paper.

Is there any thrill to equal waiting in an empty railway compartment to discover who will be one's travelling companion? Will she be a lover of log fires, and rudely healthy after Fragonard's Washerwomen or Renoir's Bougival peasants? Or will her breasts hang loose to cushion me, like Watteau's dimpled Ceres with flaxen hair full-streaming to the waist?

I get none of these—only a grey-curled, elephantine matron in the company of an emaciated lizard. Both are British, both are speaking English and both invalidate the purpose of my exile.

But noblesse oblige.

'Those cases, that rucksack—let me assist you.'

'Oh how kind!' says the fat one. 'Two damsels in distress!'

'The voice of St George!' says the other.

'Allow me to introduce myself . . .' Dash it, my good manners are unmasking me again! '. . . Tobias Mildew.'

'Mr Mildew has saved our sanity, hasn't he, Olive? If we'd had to say another word in French . . .'

'But that's why we've come, Fay! The Authority hasn't paid for us to cheat . . .'

'Authority?' I shudder at the word.

'Education. We're to pilot French into the curriculum of our eight to elevens.'

'They don't all learn it already?'

'Indeed not!' exclaims Fay.

'Wouldn't they be happier, then, to be left in peace?' I remember dull sessions with my tutors.

17

'You know you don't mean that, Mr Mildew . . .'

She has to justify their leave of absence and their special grant.

'. . . If we widen the horizons of our little ones, perhaps they won't turn out to be as insular as we are.'

'As *we* are?' queries Fay.

'As *we* are.'

'But *are* we?'

'We are.'

'Speak for yourself!'

'I shall speak for whomever I please.' She contains her irritation because of my presence. 'But Mr Mildew must think it remiss of us not to have given him our names. I'm Olive Brownlow, a Surrey headteacher for my sins. And this is Fay Passmore, my former sportsmistress and now a headteacher in her own right. Indeed her school is making quite a name for its experimental French, isn't that so, Fay?'

'In that case, we must start speaking French at once,' I protest. Both appear alarmed.

'You speak French well?' inquires Miss Passmore timidly.

'I'm afraid I do.'

'Fluently?'

'Yes.'

'You realize we're only *primary*,' puts in Miss Brownlow. 'Terribly inferior, I should think, by *your* standards.'

'Yes . . . Very small fry . . . Tiddlers, in fact.'

Miss Passmore temporarily offers small talk which I fend off in French. Soon she gives up and prattles with her partner.

'. . . I brought my own tea . . .'

'. . . I'm glad I have my warmest overcoat . . .'

'. . . I found her children's diction very poor.'

'Diction is *out* as far as I'm concerned . . .'

There is still a chance. Beside me may sit a pretty girl from Besançon who'll love me each evening when my writing quota is completed.

Again the women try to draw me:

'. . . the mysterious Mr Mildew here.'

' "The Mysterious Mr Mildew"! That appeals to me, Fay! An excellent title for a thriller!'

A Negro is examining the reservation cards. With a careless ' 'sieur 'dames' and a complaint in French about the Easter

18

crowds, he sits beside me, pressing a friendly thigh against my own. I edge away. I glance at his profile. His expression is impassive, though he has every reason to be resentful. I trust he understands the reason why I can't respond.

In embarrassment I parley with the Ladies.

'Has Dijon been offering courses to English teachers for long?'

'Dijon?'

'Dijon?'

The facts are already too apparent, but Miss Passmore expatiates:

'We're attending a cours de perfectionnement at the linguistic centre attached to Besançon University. Isn't it all so difficult to say?'

'You don't have to be so modest!' objects Olive Brownlow. 'Mr Mildew will appreciate that we teachers haven't had the same opportunities as he.'

Opportunities! Toby Mildew have opportunities! Opportunities for what, I'd like to know!

'And you, Mr Mildew,' demands Fay Passmore, 'what's the purpose of your own visit? Don't tell me you're travelling to Besançon as well!'

'That I am, Miss Passmore,' I reveal regretfully.

'Oh, drop the "Miss". Call us Fay and Olive.'

I fail to comply.

'There you are, Fay. Mr Mildew will now think we're utterly abandoned.'

'But what *is* the purpose of your visit?' Miss Passmore is determined to get her answer.

'That, I'm afraid, is the business of my Editor.'

'How evasive!'

'An unknown quantity in our midst,' adds Miss Brownlow sarcastically.

'You will have all thirty-three of us in a flutter of curiosity!'

'Now, now, Fay. We'll ask Mr Mildew no questions if he, in return, allows us to lean upon his French. Agreed, Mr Mildew?'

'Is this a threat?' I laugh with blustering falsity before retiring into frightened meditation.

The Ladies indulge in reminiscence: the Eiffel Tower, Maurice Chevalier. The Negro remains inscrutable and motionless.

I pretend to doze.

The train moves out.

'If you pass us down that bag, Mr M., you may join us in a spot of lunch.'

'I don't deny I'm on the peckish side, Miss Brownlow.'

'Oh do call us Olive and Fay!'

I partake of their tinned salmon, their chutney and chippolatas, their cherries and their cider. But I do not in payment give the right to call me Toby.

That they have not included the negro in their invitation troubles me. And it is now too late. Even were they to approach him with a smile, pride would necessitate refusal. What must he be thinking as we fiddle with the wrappings, munch and chew? What must this spurned, excluded Purple Warrior be plotting within that noble skull? A bloodbath? He sits crosslegged, ignoring me. I have been condemned with the rest—and justly.

'Why not offer some cider to our friend here?'

I crassly gesture towards him.

Their eyes signify disapproval.

Fay, the kinder of the two, wheedles, 'Monsieur, Monsieur!' as she wields the flagon.

The Purple Warrior makes no response.

'They have ears and they hear not,' mocks Olive. 'Vous voulez?' She snatches the flagon from Fay and waves it under his nose.

He examines a cuff-link.

I make another contribution:

'Vous en voudriez, Monsieur?'

No response.

'It's not worth bothering,' says Olive.

'At least we've done our best,' agrees Fay.

'They do not want to mix.'

'You sound disillusioned, Miss Brownlow.'

'Call me Olive . . . Yes I am disillusioned—or, rather, I'm a realist.'

'I have always found realists both hasty and harsh.'

'We lack charity, I fear.'

You do, Miss Passmore! So did the magistrate who sentenced me!

I change the subject.

20

'Why, Ladies, choose to pilot French as opposed to, say, Russian or Italian?'

'We do what our Authority tells us.'

'Fay's right. It calls the tune. We co-operate.'

Insuperable loneliness engulfs me, the loneliness that leads my kind to all their reckless acts of self-destruction.

We are passing chalk-pits.

'Chalk-pits but no blackboards!'

I can't resist it.

'What are those trees with mistletoe in them?' asks Fay.

'Silver birch,' says Olive.

'Mistletoe trees,' say I.

'You *are* in form, Mr M.,' says Olive.

'I meant those trees with white blossom,' says Fay.

'Almond trees,' says Olive.

'Wild cherry,' say I.

She accepts this contradiction. The teacher has become the child. I had meant to say wild plum.

'You're a mine of information, Mr Mildew. I'd have bet my bottom dollar it was apple.'

'If you knew Normandy as well as I do, Miss Passmore . . .'

'Oh, he *will* keep calling me Miss Passmore, Olive!'

'It must be wonderful to know your France, Mr M. . . . . Oh, look! Sailing!'

'Not unlike the Allier's marina.'

They stare at me askance.

'I'm the leader of the group, Mr M. I can see I shall need someone like you to keep me up to the mark.'

'Yes, where *is* the Allier?' asks Fay.

'Vichy. The war, remember?'

'Ah yes, Vichy . . .'

After Dijon I excuse myself. They move their knees to let me pass.

'I wish you'd learn to speak English, Fay. It's not "paying a call". It's "spending a penny",' I overhear.

They decide to follow my example.

'A sensible idea. Too much cider.'

'Mr Mildew was first, though, which goes to prove men have the weaker bladders.'

'Pardon Fay's vulgarity, Mr M.'

'Olive, I always said you were a prude.'

'No need to make a scene.'

Why do women of a certain age go everywhere in pairs?

The Purple Warrior and I are now alone.

'Thank you for what you did . . .'

I start in astonishment. He is speaking thick yet exact English.

'. . . You took my side against those women . . .'

'But . . .'

'No "buts". Let me shake you by the hand.'

'The cordial French custom!'

'The dirty French habit!'

'You're not a francophile?'

'Not specially. More francophone. The French Government has offered me a larger bursary to study medicine than your Commonwealth Relations Office, that is all. The powerless become mercenary. In Malawi we shall soon be short of doctors.'

'I understand.'

The Ladies return. My Purple Warrior hardens into muscular stone.

Preening, smoothing their skirts, they take their places.

'Forgive the unsavoury subject, Mr M., but, sad to relate, someone has let the side down. Dirty writing on the wall. If it weren't in English I might suspect our sooty friend here.'

'Perhaps it was one of your party,' I retort.

This confounds her. Fay giggles.

Not till Dôle does my Purple Warrior come back to life—this time to quench his thirst. He buys a bottle of lemonade from a trolley outside the window.

Dôle to Besançon. The final length of track. While the Ladies attempt to hide their disappointment at the nondescript terrain, I count the telegraph poles. The Negro drinks deeply from his bottle.

'There's nothing I dislike more than to see a person drinking from a bottle,' objects Miss Brownlow.

'We must try not to be prejudiced,' remonstrates Miss Passmore. 'If Mr Mildew here were doing it, I'm sure we wouldn't mind.'

'Mr Mildew wouldn't dream of doing such a thing. You'd

never drink straight from a bottle, would you, Mr M? Of course you wouldn't. It isn't your nature!'

My Purple Warrior, though he hasn't finished, puts the bottle on the floor beside him.

My body trembles and perspires. My face is reddening with shame. How much more of this implacable hostility can he endure without protesting?

Two minutes to five. We are nearing our destination.

I help the Ladies with their cases.

'Thank you.'

'You've been so kind and informative and helpful.'

'You're the first gentleman that's come our way in a long, long time.'

The train jolts to a halt.

Did I see aright? Could the Purple Warrior have knocked the bottle of lemonade so that its contents swilled around Miss Brownlow's feet?

'Clumsy fool! See what you've done!' she shouts.

Casting a wry glance in my direction, he is gone without a word, abandoning me to assist the Ladies down the steep steps onto the platform.

Monday, 29th April

Miss Brownlow and Miss Passmore, at the hub of a dishevelled group of fellow teachers, waved wistfuly as my taxi left for the Hôtel Europe. I do not regret my impulsive decision to spend the initial days in comfort. Hurdleford Jail provides neither telephones nor frigidaires for its inmates. The over-spending of precious francs restored me to my proper stature. At the Poker d'As around the corner I could lunch on foie gras truffe and poularde à la morille. For dinner I could sample filets de perche at the Chaland, a boat-restaurant perched on the River Doubs close by the Bregille Bridge. I use the word 'perched' advisedly. The jeu de mots conveys some measure of my contentment. Although my Editor insists that they remain unsigned, I wrote my snippets for the Monthly Arts with more enthusiasm than I had anticipated. Despite setbacks, my spirits revived.

The bars and railings of Besançon's crooked, serried buildings bristle like porcupines within a precinct girdled by the River Doubs and secured to the south by Vauban's romantic Citadelle. Nuns scurry piously along streets where soldiers rove. A drooling idiot guards a corner of the Hôtel de Ville. Students argue at tables in the Place Granvelle. Workmen play pétanque beneath the lime trees of Chamars, the former Champ de Mars. At the Centre Linguistique opposite the Faculté des Lettres in the rue Mégevand, the visiting Ladies toil genteelly at their studies.

Idyllic.

On the sloping ramparts of the Citadelle I paced a patch of sundrenched grass among the brambles, reciting poems of Herrick and Ronsard without fear of ridicule. Opposite, across the valley, stood the knoll of Chaudanne, a fortressed Mount

Athos where, two nights previously, I chased a girl among the bushes. Why did she whimper? Why panic? Why scramble from my grasp? Why spurn my well-intentioned favours? Should I seek her out again, I asked myself, to prove to her the innocence of my design? No, I must curb myself. If I quaffed too eagerly from the chalice of my freedom, I might come to believe myself divine and fall in the claws of my intoxication towards some fresh disaster. This bookworm burrower reminded himself that the tragedy of his past life is not so easily avenged. The siren wail which summons workers home at midday, the military jets from Longwy and Luxeuil which convulse at intervals the walls and panes of the redbacked town, recalled the fatal night when, long ago, I all but possessed, then lost for ever, my first and only love.

Annie signalled me. She struck a match in the stable-loft as prearranged, holding it close to the cobwebbed window so the flare would reach me at the house.

I was transformed into the surest huntsman, proud of his vigour, certain of his prize and the means of its attainment. I was fifteen. I stalked the prey that was my due.

'There is nothing to fear,' I whispered.

I sought her lips. She moved her head from side to side.

'No! No!'

I pinioned her. I tried to force myself within.

'No, no, Toby! Please not that!' She struggled. 'Toby, you are hurting me!'

She bit my arm and, raising her knee, she struck me in the groin. A plane thundered above us. Breaking free from my embrace she fled to the trap-door and stumbled down the ladder to escape me. The whining crescendo of a falling bomb tore at my eardrums. I flung myself into the hay. A roar. A streak of orange light. The timbered roof and walls juddering about me. Chaos and oblivion . . .

But I was dramatizing. I controlled myself. I looked down from beside the Citadelle into the valley of the present—at the barges, the dinky lock, the garage beside the road to Lyon. If one follows the river past the islands and the weir, one comes to a willow-shaded footbridge. This is the entrance to the Gare d'Eau, an inland harbour used by the Army's Ecole de Ponts further upstream where, at the water's edge, courtship, camaraderie, philandering and enticement converge into an ambience

25

which I was swift to recognize. Green boats, bollards, girders, a gravel expanse, did not decoy me from the hidden pulse. A girl combing her hair with studied unconcern, a soldier examining the bark of a hollow tree—these were indications of that fifth dimension which eludes the Sunday painter.

I had taken a swim there recently, and dried off in the grasses.

'A man after my own heart. But do be careful! You run the risk of warts and skin rash. The Doubs is filthy!'

I drew my towel round me and sat up. Though concealing my nakedness, I could hardly do the same for my disappointment. To have my adventure spoilt by Miss Passmore! The site became conventional again. Some harriers lumbered past. A woman rocked a pram. A boy cleaned a motorbike. Two woolly dogs chased one another's tails.

She was wearing a tracksuit bossed with badges. She did not remove her eyes from me. I was astounded at her forwardness.

'Swum yourself yet?' I tried to sound convivial.

'The piscine isn't open.'

'I meant the Doubs.'

'In *this* foul meandering thing?'

'You won't then be coming here often?'

'Not if you don't want me to.' My hopeful tone must have betrayed me. 'You seem to think I'm a manhunter. Let me assure you . . .'

She gave me to understand she would in future leave me to my privacy. But I didn't believe her. To experience the reintegration, the rebirth for which I craved, I climbed, with only stumps of mountain ash as footholds, nearer to Zeus.

The weather broke. A prey to spiritual and financial pessimism, I descended from my pinnacle to reality. I have shifted to the indifferent Hôtel Bourdaut, and eat at the university canteen and move among the common herd.

The students, as belligerent as those in England, have marred the beauty of the town with posters:

VIETNAM—First Martyred Country of the Third World War

WHAT IS BEING DONE AGAINST HUNGER IN THE WORLD?

LONG LIVE GERMAN STUDENTS
GAULLIST POWER Sacrifices Instruction, Health, Sport and Culture

I wish these callow youths would put their subsidies to better use than resorting to this kind of claptrap.

No wonder the Ladies have ceased to patronize their restaurant.

'Institutrices anglaises!' 'Quel ennui!' Supercilious cries went up at the first appearance of Miss Brownlow and her party.

They now bring packed lunches to eat at midday, and dine with their landladies. But I shall not be intimidated by intellectual dissolutes who scorn all but their own generation.

The boy who hands out the knives and forks whistles as I pass. If, at the hatch, I hesitate in choosing between cheese and a banana, I hear behind me in fretful chorus, 'Remember the queue!', 'Get a move on, slowcoach!', 'Wake up, professor!'

At the bar where one collects one's wine is a table decked with pans of left-overs, available as second helpings and referred to by the students in their argot as 'le rab'. The undergraduate couple that run the section take no pride in it. They find it no recompense to know they are contributing to the organization of a seat of learning and, consequently, to society at large. They radiate dissatisfaction. The male is dark and squat and bearded. His mate is fair and tall and spotty. She lurks behind him, a faint betrousered projection of his personality. To side with current fashion she must pretend to be his equal.

A new arrival, I put my tray upon the table while ordering my wine. The male rose to his fullest height.

'Take that off the table!'

'I beg your pardon?'

'That bloody tray! Remove it!'

'I can't. I'm getting money from my pocket.'

'I don't care what the hell you're doing!'

'Do you always use this language?'

'Yes—to obstructionists!'

'How am I obstructing you?'

'By putting a tray down *there*!'

'But whom am I obstructing?'

'Me!'

27

'The position of the tray is *not* obstructing you. It's on a table. You're beside it.'

'It's my job to see that no one puts a tray upon that table.'

'Why?'

'It interferes with those coming up for rab.'

'But at the moment there's no one here but me.'

'Remove that tray!'

'A bottle of red wine, please.'

Plaintively his partner enters the arena:

'We'll lose our job if we don't enforce the rules.'

'Rules are guides, not masters,' I explain to her.

'Ta soeur!' hissed her bearded lover.

'I protest! As a guest I do protest!'

'Circule!'

At this the spotty girl begins to snigger.

'My mother and father sacrificed their lives for the likes of you!'

'That's not our fault!' she sneers.

'Bourgeois!!' appends her homuncule.

'How dare you!' I raise my fists to challenge him. 'I am aware that that is the most insulting word in your vocabulary!'

I look for a sympathetic face among the crowd that's gathering. None do I find. Yet I am not deterred. Life has dealt me harsher blows than this young hothead could imagine.

'Come on and fight, proletarian!'

His cheeks, what I could see of them, went ashen. He did not move.

'I didn't mean to upset you,' he muttered.

'Hypocrite! Apologize!'

'I apologize.'

'I accept that apology.'

Again his girlfriend sniggers.

'And what is so funny?'

'I have the right to laugh. We women have few rights but we have the right to laugh.'

'You snigger knowing that, in the presence of your scruffy manling, you are perfectly safe!'

'No gentleman would strike a woman!'

'I have been accused of being bourgeois. Yet now you use the manners of the bourgeoisie as a defence! Double-thinking!' . . .

28

After a pause, I repeated my request for some red wine. This time I was served without demur.

I have since, though, obeyed the rule. I allow the pair to govern their puny kingdom as they please. Heaven help us all should petty tyrants such as they ever come to wield the reins of mightier power!

The student body as a whole is insupportable. It's philistine. Let someone start clanking his knife against a water-jug, and the hall is in an imitative uproar. Smugness gleams from every eye. There is kissing between mouthfuls. The girls, to prove themselves a match for their manlings, spit water and throw hunks of bread. Balancing sunglasses on their heads like grounded aviators, they spice their conversation with words like 'merde' and 'con'.

There was a time when I hankered after university, when I begrudged the opportunities of those who practised the mystiques of advanced learning. I can now rest at ease. I am proud to have played no part in these developments.

I wrote to Professor Godon of the Faculté des Lettres, enclosing a letter of introduction from my Editor. I hoped that he at least, being of my own generation, would appreciate my point of view.

We sat en quatre—father, mother, myself and sullen son— eating stuffed eggs, followed by rabbit stew and vegetable salad.

'I commend you, Madame, for this jardinière.'

She shifts uneasily.

'We eat simply,' she says.

Bobo, their mongrel dog, snarls his assent.

'It's so delightful to dine again in congenial company. I've had to endure those ill-mannered students at the Cité.'

They make no comment. I have criticised too early. Even the educated French are chauvinistic. I continue:

'Yes. Cous-cous, chicken, Yoghourt, ice-cream, wine ... I have been surprised at the excellent quality of the menus. The cous-cous, I presume, is for the benefit of your colonials.'

Madame expands. 'In France we believe in feeding our young people well.'

The professor, defensively, seizes on my reference to Empire.

'I understand the British have colonials to feed too.'

'I had not intended to discriminate. All your students are very fortunate. Yet I wonder why they, also, bite the hand that feeds them. Their manners are atrocious.'

'They have fascists for masters,' interjects the son resentfully. Mother and father laugh his remark away.

'I didn't expect to find in Besançon a replica of the situation in Berlin and London. Students should be apolitical, don't you think? I'll accept LIBERTE whitewashed on the walls. But DUTSCHKE! I have been offended. The agitators at Nanterre have much to answer for. It was they, wasn't it, who first sent this wave of unrest rippling across your country?'

'Unrest!' expostulated the son. 'You call an attempt at dialogue a frank protest calling for democratization, "unrest"!'

'I do.'

'I would prefer to call our campaign a religious movement—'

Monsieur le Professeur swiftly interrupts:

'Students apart, you find our city to your liking?'

'I dislike the sound of jets. I dislike the midday siren. I am reminded of the war.'

Another subject that's taboo.

'Have you managed to work despite the noise? Are all the facilities you require available? Is the Fac Library to your satisfaction?'

'I have borrowed several works of reference.'

'I'd be interested if you named a few. Your editor is said to be the hardest of taskmasters!'

I mentioned Claud Fohlen's 'Histoire de Besançon', Coindre's 'Mon Vieux Besançon' and Lucien Febvre's 'Histoire de Franche-Comptée'.

Madame offers me more rabbit. Again she apologizes for the frugality of the repast. 'With such a large family . . .' She looks around but, in Bobo, husband and son, fails to find sufficient confirmation of her statement. 'There is also my daughter, Antoinette. Maybe you could help her with her Bac.'

'Her English texts are very American!' jokes the professor.

Money and sweet company—the suggestion is irresistible:

'Too happy, only too happy . . .'

'We must decide on a fee,' adds the professor.

'No fee,' I object unwisely, forgetting parsimonious Madame will concur.

'How very generous of you, Mr Mildew!'

Whereupon she repeats her offer of more rabbit.

'Drink up!' urges Professor Godon, plying me with ordinaire.

'Hadn't you better consult Antoinette!' growls the son.

'Robert!!' His mother apologizes in a fluster: 'Antoinette will be back soon from the pictures. She will be charmed to meet you and have a preliminary chat.'

Robert throws down his fork, kicks back his chair and stamps out of the room.

Again Madame apologizes:

'The young are very much in two minds at present. You are not the only object of their spleen. Papa has been insulted in mid-lecture, haven't you, dear?'

'You will understand, Mr Mildew, that my position prevents me discussing university matters with outsiders.'

'Quite, quite.' And, while Madame goes in search of the dessert, I pass the last of my meat to Bobo.

Madame returns with strawberries. Robert walks behind her carrying a jug of cream. He has been ordered to make communication, for he proceeds to quiz me.

'What do you like reading best?'

'Balzac. I have a passion for Balzac.'

My Editor refused to let me review the Maurois 'Life'.

'Not Barillon, Cohn-Bendit, Viansson-Ponté . . .?'

'I am a literary animal, not a political one.'

'You are not interested in our causes, then?'

'Such delicious strawberries, Madame. What was that? Oh, I'm far too busy, Robert, I'm afraid, for "causes".'

'Doing what, for example?'

'You *are* a dog that worries his bones. Well, let me see. I've been exploring your town. And I've been enabling a group of British ladies find their feet here. I have even accompanied them on some of their excursions. They need a friend and an adviser... I'd love another helping of those strawberries.'

'You mean those old mares at the Centre de Linguistique Appliquée?'

'Pass your plate, Mr Mildew!' his mother intervenes. 'And Robert, don't be so rude! One day you'll be old yourself!'

'Mr Mildew, are you prepared to sign a petition on behalf of some students wrongly accused of theft?'

31

'It is not so much wrongful accusations that are to be feared, Robert, as wrongful convictions.'

The professor is in full agreement. 'Well said, Mr Mildew!'

'Are you prepared to sign?' Robert insists.

'I am no lover of the police, but I would have to know the facts.'

'Well then . . .'

He is about to tell the story. His parents, though, have heard it far too often. They cut him short.

'It is very late, Robert.'

'Papa is right. Mr Mildew must be tired. He is a very busy man.'

Robert sulks. I am aware that I have been unjust.

'It is not that the problems of the young do not interest me, Robert. It is what they say and do about them.'

No comment. He has taken offence once more. I wish his sister would arrive.

Headlights of cars sweep through Chamars, then across the Doubs and up past the house.

Madame Godon believes she is interpreting my thoughts:

'Sad, isn't it? We chose the rue des Germinettes to be on the Chaudanne side and, within two years, we found ourselves plagued by endless traffic using the new bridge and highroad! But now you must sample my beignets de carnaval. Open the Mousseux, papa!'

She has perfumed her floury fritters with orange essence. I wash away the taste.

There is also cherry pie.

The professor raises the tenor of the conversation:

'What a shame our museum is closed for renovations. Its Courbets are magnificent.'

'The museum at Ornans, I understand, is rich in Courbets. I prefer Fragonard. His "Rosalie" here in Besançon would have pleased me immeasurably, but I see I shall have to compromise. A little bread is better than no water.'

'I happen to consider Courbet the more substantial.'

I leave him with the last word.

We move to have coffee in a semi-circle round an empty hearth. A potted philodendron climbs the wall. There are

Dresden china soldiers on the mantelpiece. I can find no books. I seize on a print of the Citadelle.

'The Citadelle to my mind is the glory of Besançon. Do you recall that moment in "Le Rouge et le Noir" when Julien Sorel, arriving from Switzerland, surveys it for the very first time?'

'Cointreau or Bisquit?'

'Bisquit . . . For me it stands for order, endurance, the value of tradition . . .'

The door bursts open. The room fills with the seductive exhalations of an ardent pulchritude. I am introduced to Antoinette.

I recognize her. She recognizes me. She is the girl I chased upon Chaudanne! I am the man who tried to embrace her in the darkness!

'Our friend Mr Mildew has kindly offered to help you with your English texts,' her father tells her.

'I know them off by heart.'

'Yes, but he can correct your weak pronunciation.'

'Not on your life!'

'Antoinette!!' both her parents remonstrate in unison.

Robert is delighted.

'Say sorry to Mr Mildew at once!!!' Madame Godon is in a tearful temper.

'All right, all right! I'm sorry!'

Why has she relented...? Will she not, after all, betray me? Is she afraid I may report the fact I've seen her strolling in a manner calculated to invite advances?

'I shall think no more of your misdemeanour,' I say pointedly.

'I'm going out now, if you don't mind.'

'Really Antoinette! You've only just come in! What's the matter with you this evening? Mr Mildew, how can I make amends?'

'Bobo needs his run. Someone has to take him.'

'I don't know what to say, Mr Mildew. I think, perhaps, in her present frame of mind it *would* be best if she went, don't you? Very well, then. Go! But wrap up properly and don't go as far as the summit tonight. Bobo will catch cold as well as you. We can't afford one invalid, let alone two.'

'You allow her to walk alone upon Chaudanne?' I ask when she has left.

'As a university professor I assure you that the young can no longer be imprisoned. Our resident students are already demanding to be allowed to sleep together, never mind taking dogs for walks! Antoinette, if she passes the Bac, will be a student herself in the autumn. What will we be able to say to her then? Better, perhaps, to be prepared for the worst. Someone, I gather, insulted her the other evening. A timely lesson—though, if I caught the blackguard, I'd flog the life out of him.'

My heart quails.

'She certainly doesn't seem to relish the idea of me as tutor.' I rise to go, feigning displeasure to conceal my anxiety. 'You, like me, are busy people with a busy day ahead of you. I trust that I have not outstayed my welcome.'

'By no means, Mr Mildew!' protests Madame Godon, almost running to fetch my coat and hat.

We shake hands in the hall.

I wave as I walk away. My legs are trembling. What if Antoinette talks? What if her parents call the police? She will be pondering what to do as she walks, as I am walking, beneath the rain. By the time she returns she will have made her decision. When I reach the Bourdaut, the police may be already waiting . . .

In the Brasserie Granvelle the voice of Georgette Plana on the juke-box, singing 'Je m'aprelle Frisson', drowns the words from the television in the corner. Students, our leaders of the future, are working flipper machines and playing 'babyfoot'. Others kiss and fondle.

I choose a table at the window. A girl is seated there alone. I make conversation:

'Isn't the view deceiving? The benches, the bandstand beyond, the looped lights of the Palais de la Bière, give the impression of a rainswept seaside resort . . .'

Impatiently she drums her fingers.

I leave her free to supplement her grant. I prefer to be drenched than to consort with wasters. I prefer the soughing torrents, the splurging gutters of the inky world outside to the updated facilities of a teenage whore-house. And so my feet bear me, a willing victim, through night's phosphorescent cavern of pre-determined disappointments.

I shelter in the pissotière of the Hôtel de Ville. I read its messages, seeking comfort from those like myself who, because the suspicious have snatched away their crock of gold, have slid down a rainbow to perdition. These men, homosexuals for the most part, rejected as I am for instincts natural to themselves, of the same age as I am and therefore doubly repellent to their enemies, find in this rude enclosure an outlet for their hankerings and, in a private corner which no one else need scrutinize, inscribe their hopes and fears and fantasies.

I add my version of frustrated virtue and pass on. Au revoir, my friends. May you one day find your assorted havens. If not, death will seem to you the sweetest haven of them all.

Past the Hôtel Europe. Past the Post Office. Into another flooded refuge by the Pont St Pierre. Is that a girl I see undressing in the Officers' Quarters of the Barracks? Is her shamelessness an invitation? Hers is the only window now alight in Besançon. Does she see me peering at her over the cement partition? I walk into the street. I gaze up at her golden signal. A Robin Hood, I show Maid Marion my quiver. She draws the curtains. I return to the urinal. Now there is laughter there. Its Fairies dance around me in a ring. They tease me. They do not mock. Bless the little Fairies. They understand. They know what happens at the witching hour. They, too, are mesmerized.

'Hands off! Hands off!' I tell them. 'You are not for me. My demons are not your demons. We worship at different altars. Away! Away!'

Peals of tinkling laughter.

'Naughty, naughty!' I cry.

'Less naughty than you!'

They jump on tiptoe, their jewelled hands glinting in the prism of a moonbeam to allure me.

'Come with us!'

'Heigh-ho!'

'Tra-la!'

'Flibbertygibbety!'

'Upsadaisy!'

'Here is true freedom! Here is happiness!'

'Long life O Quean!'

I protest: 'I am not one of your number! I must leave you!'

'We shall follow! We shall follow!'

The Hôtel des Bains and the Casino sleep huddled in one another's arms. A man probes the sodden earth beneath the wailing trees of the Promenade Micaud. He shines a torch into my face.

'Looking for worms?' I ask.

'I was until you scared them off.'

By day, the Promenade Micaud is suited to the Ladies. They are impressed by such embellishments as its swan and Tuscan Folly, its waterfall and grotto, its flowerbeds and jeux d'enfants. There they can sit upon some bench in the certainty that some desperate stranger will accost them, whereupon, in the safety of daylight, they can walk disgustedly away, happy to know that to someone in this world they are not repulsive.

After dusk, the place becomes a dome for discreet copulation and cavortings. I have often waited there, hoping some maiden would approach me.

Tonight the swan is motionless upon its moat made choppy by the downpour. I have never seen this swan to move. It never inspects the wooden nest upon its island. It never bends to drink. It never flies away. Have its wings been clipped as mine have? Is it, in adversity, as powerless as I? A marble symbol of impressive fortitude, it floats mysterious, inscrutable and dignified, an inspiration at this time of sorrow when, a man in my prime, I must haunt the shadows for fear that Antoinette may have set the wheels of Law turning relentlessly against me.

Again I hear those tinkling peals of laughter. They've followed me! The jewelled dwarfs, the merry wanderers, are trooping through the trees towards me. Unbuttoning their frilly shirts to give their pigeon chests a shower-bath, they encircle me and chant temptations.

'We cost so little and, look, we're everything you want!'

I sneeze.

'Let us warm away that cold of yours!'

A bird creaks like a door above us.

'I'm sorry if I tempted you.'

They take it up in chorus. 'Tempt *us*!' They give themselves airs. They grimace. I move to break their ranks. They bar the way.

The police, the Godons, the students—what is there to fear compared with this?!

'I shall call for help!'

'At this hour!'

'I shall call the worm collector!'

They raise imaginary hats. They bow and curtsey. They let me pass.

I slink to my hotel.

The police were not awaiting me. It is four o'clock, and I am weary with writing. The rain still sputters against the panes. Soon the patron will sweep his courtyard and trundle the dust-bins on a trolley to the street. When his daughter, dainty and fawnlike, brings me my tray, I will touch her smooth, bare arms. There is no risk I would not run to be loved by such a darling.

3

Saturday, 4th May

A therapeutic word about the Ladies.

What they claim to be chance meetings have given them excuse to use and cosset me.

'Nec juvenis nec pulchra' adequately describes the group. Its leader, Olive Brownlow, tells me she was elected by democratic vote. Fay Passmore, when she is not touring the river banks, only leaves her side to be 'indisposed'. One moves spirally outwards from this Concentre through a self-appointed Inner Circle to what may be dubbed the Outer Pale whose main concern is where to find tea made with boiling water.

The Concentre and the Inner Circle have adopted me as guide and mentor.

'My niece has married an architect in Ohio. How much is the stamp on a postcard to America?'

'Can you recommend a Swiss hotel near the border? I feel it's wicked not ever to use my car.'

'Which dictionary do you prefer?'

I have helped where I can. 'To be of service' is my motto. I realize they laugh at me behind my back—Miss Brownlow found me staring at some lace-edged lingerie in Innovation—but I am cleverer, more desperate than they are; I shall have the last of the laughs if I get my way.

'Tut tut, Mr M. There's no accounting for tastes!'

I gave not the slightest indication of embarrassment, but merely inquired if she and the rest of the Ladies were benefiting from their course and if their lodgings were satisfactory.

'The outings are the best. We go together in a coach. Perhaps you'd sometimes care to join us. After all, you were so helpful to us with our cases and, as party leader, I would have no difficulty introducing you.'

I accepted. Maybe, on return to England, they will introduce me to some of their past pupils. They praise my devotion to the culture of France and its people. I do not disillusion them.

'Everything comes so easily to you, Mr Mildew!'

Forgive me if I laugh a hollow laugh.

But I forget. Beware of vanity! They flatter because they want to use me as congenial companion, interpreter, complainer, inquirer, encyclopaedia and general factotum. I shall play their game, live up to their requirements when it suits me. So long as I remember that they and their kind support the magistrate who sentenced me, why not form a temporary alliance to my advantage?

'*Such a gentleman*!' This means I cater for your every whim. As you place a cigarette between your lips, I fumble for my matches. I also open doors, incline or half rise or raise a hat when you appear. I murmur 'After you!' I feign excitement at your latest frowsy dress. Such taste! Such charm! Such je ne sais quoi! I miscalculate your ages. Fifty-five?! Impossible! Quite impossible! I carry parcels, adapt to your pace, agree your arms have caught the sun, that times have changed, that money's lost its value. I say, 'May I have the pleasure?', 'Would you be so good as to . . .?' I allow you to nag, and I never give a quid pro quo. I never smile at a vulgar innuendo, but signal a 'compris' from perceiving eyes. I never argue, pursue an idea, take sides. I simplify. I inquire are you too hot, too cold, and shall I shut the window. I lead you by the elbow across the street. I walk in front of you up steps, I catch hold of you as you descend to make the landing gracefully balletic.

'*I wish I'd his brain*!' I can recite poetry and prose verbatim. I remember dates, streets, rates of exchange, the names of restaurants and drinks. I deliver information without pause for reflection. I have read the notices. I speak faultless French, and we are not in Russia.

'*Must be worth a fortune*!' I took a taxi from the station to the Hôtel Europe. I eat fastidiously. Waiters obey. I polish my shoes and press my trousers. My cuffs and collars are clean. I wear turn-ups, and I use my hat with confidence. I take *The Times*. I distinguish my consonants. I have travelled the length

39

and breadth of France—and we are not in Russia. In other words, I have learned on a failed freelance's income and tuppence worth of debenture dividends how to outstare . . .

Selfish, easily impressed old bags! I must grin and bear you! At least, regarding my possible relations with the Law, you will cloak me in respectability.

'Fine weather for the ducks, Mr Mildew!'

In rain the Ladies retire at lunchtime to the cellar restaurant of the Faculté des Lettres. I have heard the Outer Pale, among pseudo-intellectuals completing the Le Monde crossword, sing 'Tiptoe Through the Tulips' at full throat while beating time with forkfuls of salami and cole slaw.

On sunny days they eat from bags in the Place Granvelle.

'Have an oatmeal biscuit!'

'Have a bite of Cadbury's from home!'

'Just in time for some nice hot tea from the thermos!'

'But, Ladies, I'd prefer to experiment with the specialities of the region!'

'Nonsense, Mr M.!'

I make a final bid: 'Have you any cancoillotte?'

In saving the cost of another lunch, I become embroiled, place myself under yet another obligation.

'There now. Serviette, knife, plate. Tear yourself a piece of bread. Oh, isn't this the real McCoy, sitting in a French square eating French things like conk-whatever-it-is with the author of "The Hunchback" looking on!'

'I can't see why they've got him in a toga. With quotations underneath from "Les Feuilles d'Automne", wouldn't a fig-leaf be more appropriate? Forgive my sense of humour!'—that's Wendolyn Moxey, an amateur actress who asks to be called Wendy. 'All the folks call me Wendy, so why don't you?'

'Here's to L'Ecole Nationale d'Industrie Laitière de Marmirolle!' I say. That was where they bought the cheese—on one of their excursions.

'What a mouthful!' cries Miss Moxey. 'Sorry everyone! That wasn't supposed to be a pun!' She pulls a face and holds her forehead.

The professor who showed us round the college had black greasy hair and a broken tooth. His fifty-six pupils—all under twenty—

are men, with one notable exception. His eyes studied mine intently as he spoke of her. Did we share a common interest? 'Where is she today?' I asked off-handedly. 'I do not know,' he answered. 'Perhaps she is ill. This inclement Jura weather . . .' He veered to another subject. Was she his mistress?

'An excellent buy!' I praise the cancoillotte.

Ecstasy. Hands reaching for knives and second helpings.

'I knew you'd like it, Mr Mildew. Why didn't you get some?'

'It doesn't always keep. I haven't a fridge at my new hotel.'

'You had one at the Europe?'

'Most certainly.'

'You're quite out of our class.'

Yes, Mr M., you're quite out of our class.'

'Where are you staying now?'

'The Hôtel des Bains,' I lie. I don't want them snooping.

Miss Farley of Bath is jealous. 'I can't stand the plastic flowers there. Nor the watch display behind the bar.'

Mrs Slatter of Bradford is suspicious. 'Why eat your grub, then, at the Cité?'

'To avoid the watch display and the plastic flowers!'

Laughter.

Mrs Slatter, however, though she says 'too shay', does not appear to be convinced.

Mrs Slatter, the Purple Warrior and I found ourselves together recently in the Maison de la Presse. She was all sweetness till he'd gone. Then, browsing through a *Woman's Own*, she made her attitude clearer.

'The likes of him will soon be cutting us up in the hospitals.'

'Yes, many negroes *are* qualifying as surgeons.'

'I wish when they were qualified they'd run back up the trees they came from!'

'But with our own doctors emigrating . . .'

'I'd rather die.'

'Rubbish. I'm surprised at you. With so much to contribute as a teacher . . .'

'You should have seen how one of those apes treated my mother when she fell and split her head on the rim of a bucket. Stitched her up he did without so much as offering an anaesthetic. Sadistic bastard!'

'They, necessarily, have been trained to a more heroic view of suffering.'

'But my mother hasn't. An old lady of eighty! No anaesthetic! I ask you!'

'Maybe it was you who resented it more than your mother.'

At this she lapsed from standard English into Yorkshire.

'Daft brush! We'll never get on the same wires. For corn, Mr Mildew, you take the crumpet! Niggers should only be allowed to treat their nigger brothers.'

'Where would we be if everyone thought as you? The buses . . .'

She wouldn't budge.

'They should never have been let in.'

'Nonsense, woman!' My blood was up. 'They're just what our young girls need!'

She looked at me incredulously.

'Come on, Mr Mildew! Let's go for a cup of tea!'

Feeling as she did, how could she invite me! Feeling as I did, how could I accept!

The Ladies take tea at Maison Décombe. Its tartan wall-paper, hung with prints of British hunting scenes, gives them security. Strange how 'tally-ho!' abroad appeals to those who take only a theoretic interest in the blood sports. These women would probably be the first to sigh 'Poor fox!' at home.

The cakes are admired, chosen and paid for in an ante-room. From here they are ceremoniously carried to a table, then quartered, relished and ingested. The tulipes massepains must wilt, the Choux Chantilly turn a little sour, the religieuses cross themselves internally at the arrival of their dreaded customers. I almost hear the tartelettes swearing.

'Take your pick, Mr Mildew.'

'Une figue de pâte d'amande.'

'I'll have whatever-he-said, too.'

I repeat 'une figue de pâte d'amande' for the benefit of the assistant.

Mrs Slatter insists on paying. Which is just as well. I'll need every spare franc if I'm to last my time here. I protest, though, effusively.

'This is about the only place in Besançon I don't feel proper queer in,' she confesses loudly.

'Why?'

'They do a pot. None of those bloody tea-bags on a string for Sarah! There's Alice!!'

She waves to Miss Farley of Bath. Miss Farley's christian name is Alicia. Northern accents grate upon her delicate sensibilities. She examines her bracelet. She makes it plain she does not today wish to be reminded of mines, factories, pop groups and bingo.

'Come on, luv! There's a seat here beside Mr Mildew!'

'Ah! Mr Mildew!'

That has changed her attitude. She has more than a sneaking regard for my polish and civility, just as Sarah Slatter has deep down for hers.

She finds a waiter to carry her tea things.

'How naice to see you, Mr Mildew! I thought that after our day in Amancey when one of our number ran from a pigsty with a handkerchief held to her nose you would refuse to consort with us again!'

'I am not so petty, Miss Farley. Large Whites, weren't they?'

'Dirty Great Browns more like!' bellows Mrs Slatter. 'Rolling in their own muck!'

'All raight! All raight! No need—I use your pet expression—to turn blue at the gills!' intercepts Miss Farley, glancing in my direction.

'Thanks a bundle! You aren't always that ladylike yourself when you've had a knock of the brandy! You nearly did a monkey's because the coach driver wouldn't drop you at your door. What was it you called him? A "ruddy collaborator"?'

'Ladies! Ladies!'

'I said it behind his back, not to his face! Sorry, Mr Mildew! You must find all this extremely boring. Have you heard that, in a trench beneath the cellars of the Pump Room in Bath, Professor Barry Cunliffe of Southampton University has discovered some Samian pottery, imported from France; also the corner of a lunar pediment and a . . .'

The day at Amancey was arranged under the auspices of the Committee for International Exchanges. Maps on knee, we took to the Pontarlier Road as morning mists rolled upwards from the Doubs, unfolding bridges, cargo boats, cranes and woodpiles. The Citadelle floated like Valhalla above the Faubourg Rivotte.

43

As Wendolyn Moxey declared loudly, 'Covent Garden couldn't have done better.'

There had been the customary race to get the seat beside me. Another Lady of the Inner Circle, Miss Isobel Westbright of South Kensington, won by a narrow margin.

She is as eager for culture as Miss Farley. She is also too eager in other ways.

'When we arrive back in London we must go to the National Film Theatre together. They show some wonderful French films. I've seen most of the nouvelle vagues there.'

'I don't belong.'

'Be my guest, then. I presume you belong to the Institut.' I pretend not to hear. I am not going to have her spoil my evenings there.

'I said I presume you belong to the Institut Français.'

'Never presume anything, dear lady!'

'It's only five minutes from my flat.'

My heart sinks.

'Same with the V & A. I wonder if you love the Jones Collection as much as I do? If you paid me a penny for every time I'd visited *that*, I'd be a very, very rich girl indeed!'

I am irritated. 'There are better rooms. The ceramics . . .'

The student guide is spewing facts. His louche lips almost touch the microphone. Sight of the Citadelle was his cue to relate the history of Besançon from the era of bêtes sauvages to Vauban and Louis XIV.

Olive Brownlow taps my shoulder from behind. 'What's he saying?'

From over the aisle, Wendolyn Moxey passes me a scrap of paper on which she's scrawled, 'Je ne comprends pas. Help!'

Miss Westbright beside me does not give in so easily. She is watching the scenery in a studied manner which the guide, who cannot see her, is intended to read as 'Don't go on and on so! Let us first absorb it *visually*.'

I go up to the guide and whisper in his ear. He returns the microphone to its hook and I earn my passage by making a short summary in English of what he has been saying. When I have finished, he substitutes the radio for the sound of his own voice. The Rolling Stones are appropriately singing '2000 Light Years From Home'.

'Thank you, Mr Mildew.'

'Very well done!'

'What a brain!'

'What good luck you discovered him, Olive! Or was it Fay?'

Fay Passmore isn't on the present trip. She is 'indisposed'.

'We'd be lost without you, Mr M.!'

'Would you shut the window in the roof?'

I comply, obstructing the current of clear, fresh air I'd been enjoying.

My exaggerated 'A vos services, Mesdames!' raises a popular laugh.

Miss Westbright, still scanning the countryside, probes me for facts about myself to communicate, no doubt, to the rest in private afterwards.

'The others believe you are here on some personal mission.'

'I review books, write the occasional endpiece . . .'

'There's nothing more to it than that? Some kind of an escape, perhaps?'

'Your drift eludes me.'

'Has someone hurt you very deeply?'

'Is there anyone alive, Miss Westbright, who hasn't been hurt?'

'You admit it!'

I am uneasy.

'Admit what?' I know this dialogue so well. 'Tell me your own story, Miss Westbright.'

'Oh, it would bore you to distraction!'

There you are! All take and no give, these women who go round pouring oil. To discover a weakness lends them importance. But they won't let you near their own for fear of forfeiting superiority. And what would be the use of sharing a particle of the truth with Miss Westbright? What could she do to help? Her pained expression of understanding would bury Annie more deeply in the grave.

'Miss Westbright, do you enjoy teaching?'

'I'd prefer not to talk shop. Would you like an apple?'

'Very much.'

'Did you take breakfast this morning?'

I nod.

'Promise!'

Why on earth should I promise?

'I promise.'

'Well I can only hope you haven't got your fingers crossed. My brother is a bachelor. With no one to cook for him he's inclined not to bother about food. The result is . . .'

Assumptions, assumptions!

'Do I look like a man who doesn't eat, Miss Westbright?' She runs an eye over my corporation.

'A little bit of this and a little bit of that, probably adding up to too much starch . . .'

Will she never stop!

'. . . my brother . . .'

I switch my attention to the radio. It's preferable to a calorie by calorie account of the diet of the brother of Miss Westbright.

Tom Jones is singing:

> My my my Delilah
> Why why why Delilah . . .

Soon, interpreting a brutal song of murder as though it were 'Daisy Daisy', most of the Ladies are participating in the chorus.

> So be*fore* they come to break down the *door*
> For*give* me Delilah I *just* couldn't take any mo-ore.

Startling magpies to left and right, the coach lurches onwards.

'. . . If there's any sewing I can do for you. I know how difficult my brother finds that side of things.'

'Thank you. I'll bear your kind offer in mind. Buttons often *are* a problem.'

'I could come to your hotel.'

And find I'm not at the Hôtel des Bains . . . Perhaps I'd better tell her now that I'm at the Bourdaut. But would she not say to her friends, 'You should have seen his room! Holes in the curtains. Walls a murky brown. Lino on the floor. Tepid water. No proper facilities for drying socks and smalls . . .'? No, I don't want her pity.

The guide is blowing into the microphone to test its efficacy. To punish the Ladies for my previous interruption, he resumes his story in faster-than-ever French:

'We have now moved off the N.67 towards the Miroir de Scey—a truly delightful (he winks at the driver) reach of still water on a tributary of the River Loue. We shall stop there for ten minutes of photography, after which we shall remount and proceed to Scey-en-Varais from where we shall climb on foot to the Châtelet St Denis. No doubt Mesdames, Mesdemoiselles, et le Monsieur, will by then have sufficient appetite to enjoy the lunches prepared for us by the peasants of Amancey.'

He spits out the word 'peasants'. I have nothing against the word but, from him, I would prefer 'farmers'.

He hasn't finished.

'. . . The peasants of France, as opposed to the town dwellers, are miserly and suspicious of strangers such as you (another wink to the driver)—so beware!'

'What on earth was all *that* about?'

Again I am called on to translate.

'Do you take Vitamin tablets?' Miss Westbright resumes.

At least by stopping at the Miroir I'll be able to change my seat. In exasperation I take my book down from the rack and occupy my mind with *La Fille aux Yeux d'Or*.

'Doesn't reading in a bus give you a headache?'

I am photographed over half a dozen times at the water's edge. My picture in the British Sundays probably lines the shelves of their larders.

'THE MOST DISGUSTING CASE WHICH HAS COME BEFORE ME IN MANY YEARS' SAYS MAGISTRATE

'Just the sort of place my mother would choose to do in oils. I believe it's known as the Désespoir du Peintre!'

'My father would enjoy the fishing. See that trout leap? Anyone know when the season starts?'

Click. I am snapped once more.

'Got you! How much is the negative worth?!'

I pretend to be engrossed in a buttercup.

Back in the bus I choose an empty seat. Such is her confidence and curiosity, Isobel Westbright moves her position to join me.

'How wise to sit away from the sun! Have another apple! . . . Have you always been a Londoner, Mr Mildew?'

'I spent my childhood in Oxfordshire. The rest has been London.'

I hope this satisfies her. I don't intend to tell her of the orphanage, or my trips to France which led to my entanglement with the French side of the Monthly Arts.

'Oxfordshire! How I envy you! The war hardly touched there, did it? I was one of the Blitz children. I vouch for those Henry

Moore drawings of the crowds sheltering in the Underground. Whereabouts do you live at the moment?'

'Notting Hill.'

She takes an address book from her bag.

I give her the street but I lie about the number.

'Telephone?'

'No telephone.'

Also untrue.

'Never mind. I won't forget to contact you. Cross my throat.'

'I'm hard to pin down. To read I must have silence. To have silence I must work while others sleep.'

'You fortunate man! To have retained your ideals! To do work for which you have a passion!'

'Aren't you a teacher?'

'Disillusioned, Mr Mildew! Disillusioned!'

Below the Châtelet St Denis is a church. The graveyard is a livid furnace of plastic chrysanthemums.

Crickets whistle in a field. I overhear an argument:

'Crickets.'

'No, cicadas!'

The Ladies retire discreetly into the woods to answer nature's calls.

American tourists are up at the castle.

'An eeooblee-ye-e-e-et?'

'Yeah, buddy! An eeooblee-yet.'

'Pretty neat, I guess.'

I take a Lady's arm across a rickety bridge.

'Such good manners! Whatever his faults, he has good manners!'

So they think I've faults!

Local dignitaries shake our hands as we descend at Amancey. A band of schoolchildren plays bugles and a drum. We march behind it in procession to a café where, over wine, we introduce ourselves and are applauded.

'My name is Alicia Farley. I make an omelette (Mr Mildew, how do you say "second to none"?), I make an omelette second to none. My age is a secret. I live in Bath, a watering place famous for its architecture and its music.'

'I'm a butcher,' announces one of our hosts to the merriment of the student guide.

48

'My name is Isobel Westbright. I live in London. I am unmarried. I cannot continue. I haven't the words.'

She sits down abruptly in an aura of confusion.

The girls in the band are helpless in one corner.

Now for Olive Brownlow. Very much the figurehead, she explains that she teaches French in order to revive the entente cordiale between our two great countries.

Prolonged ovation.

Our chief host rises.

'My family and my wife's family have been peasants for more than three generations. I own the finest herd of Montbeliards in the region. I milked them this morning at six o'clock. You, my guests, may watch me milk them, if you so desire, this evening at six forty-five. Needless to say, I shall not be wearing this unsoiled suit in which I have clothed myself to welcome you. But I shall be wearing it again tonight at eight o'clock in my own granary when I preside at the Soirée d'Amitié to which you are all invited—'

Cheers and banging of tables.

'I raise my glass to our charming English guests. Santé!'

Santé! Santé! The word echoes and re-echoes till it dwindles to a last shy grunt.

It is the task of the negro-hater, Sarah Slatter of Bradford, to follow that.

She alludes to the grand young people of today. She is married with four fine boys. The youngest is engaged to a Parisian model.

The din which reigns following this announcement causes her to lose her nerve. She, too, uncertain whether she is being mocked or encouraged, sits down abruptly.

Next, I explain I am 'an intruder'. There are cries of 'Nonsense!', 'An asset!', 'We'd be lost without you!' I am at Besançon, I particularize, to benefit from its two libraries—the Bibliothèque Municipale and the Bibliothèque de l'Université. But it is occasions such as this which alleviate the arduous duties of the scholar. I am indebted not only to our hosts but to these lovely ladies who have asked me to become their friend.

'Bien dit, bien dit!' the butcher cries. My health is drunk by all the company. 'Bien dit!' 'Bien dit!' ...

And so the round continued. Patsy Jones—a Siamese cat-breeder and Moral Rearmer from Petworth—Wendolyn Moxey, the amateur actress . . . There was also a potter, a golfer, a folk-dancer—all the English enthusiasms were represented.

After which, Patsy Jones and myself were hustled off by a 'peasant' in his Peugeot to lunch with his well-heeled wife and children.

'I congratulate you, Mr Mildew, on your excellent French. Am I right when I say I detect traces of Provence?'

I could not forgive him that, despite a subsequent tour of neighbouring waterfalls and springs. I have always prided myself on my Parisian accent.

Rose-patterned oilcloths gleamed in the granary that night beneath paraffin lamps and dancing candle-flames. Pine-branches and streamers bedecked the walls. We stared at one another, villagers and strangers, between bunches of narcissi and bottles of wine and orangeade.

A bugler of the band dressed in kingfisher blue squeezed beside me. As the evening proceeded, her natural gaiety stripped away my prudence. I placed my hand inside her dress. I asked her to conduct me round the farmyard. We sauntered arm in arm to the sound of distant music. I attempted a further familiarity. She unaccountably took fright.

We returned. Her disordered raven hair was a memento of my near success. The assembled company was chanting:

Un, deux, trois, quatre, cinq, B!
Un, deux, trois, quatre, cinq, R!
Un, deux, trois, quatre, cinq, A!
Un, deux, trois, quatre, cinq, V!
Un, deux, trois, quatre, cinq, O!
Un, deux, trois, quatre, cinq, BRAVO!

as if to welcome us. Relaxed by the wine, even the Ladies of Bath and Bradford had forgotten their differences.

A cowbell rang for silence. The Deputy Mayor spoke.

'Quick, Mr M.!'

I scribbled out some words in reply for Olive Brownlow. 'Service' is my motto.

Sarah Slatter, not to be outdone (Was she aspiring to the leadership?), called for Auld Lang Syne. Several of the bewildered French did a knees-bend instead of crossing hands.

We swayed tipsily towards the coach. The Ladies were presented by the farmers' wives with narcissi from the vases. My bugler girl was clutched round the waist by a hefty bumpkin as she waved to me.

'Au revoir!'

'C'était magnifique!'

Settling. Sighing sadly.

'Vous êtes contentes?' from the guide.

'Wee *weee*! *Tray* contentes!'

Then the post mortem as our hermetic world on wheels raced homewards past farmhouses blinded to our existence by bars and shutters:

'The only thing I didn't like was the bugling band.'

'The welcome was touching. But they didn't have to play at dinner.'

'That song the schoolmaster sang must have been risky! Who was it by, Mr M.?'

'Brassens.'

'Brass who?'

'My host at lunchtime showed me his pigs. Whew what a pong!'

'Mine plied me with booze. With*out* success.'

'Oh, you're dreadful!'

'Well, let's face it, men are beasts!'

'I doubt if Mr Mildew agrees with that, do you, Mr Mildew?'

'Present company excepted?'

This goes down well.

I am sitting with Miss Patsy Jones, the Siamese cat-breeder and Moral Rearmer. She thanks me for supporting her at lunchtime.

'I'd have been lost without your social expertise. Though didn't you rather blot your escutcheon this evening with that bugler girl in kingfisher blue? After all, she couldn't have been more than a schoolgirl!'

'You're not suggesting . . .'

'I was not impressed . . . but, as you were so open, I'm inclined to trust you. I just thought I'd mention it. Now that the air's been cleared we can be friends again.'

She coughs fitfully. The effort of speaking her fears aloud has plainly been too much for her.

Olive Brownlow is touring with a money-box.

'Seventeen francs!!' complains Miss Farley.

'Oh come, come, Alice! It was well worth it!'

'Seventeen francs for Old MacDonald's Farm, potato soup, vegetable salad, frankfurters, cheap wine and a couple of stupid songs!'

'The *lunch* was free.'

'I realize the lunch was free. That's why I'm complaining!'

'But if they charged for the lunch the cost would be *more* than seventeen!'

'They *didn't* charge for the lunch, Olive. Don't you get the point?'

She pays nonetheless.

I search tendentiously for my wallet.

'No, Mr M.! I wouldn't dream of asking.'

'I insist.'

'We won't hear of Mr M. paying, will we?' she calls to everyone.

'No!', 'No!', 'No!'—and they all, including Miss Farley, contribute extra francs.

I continue to protest.

'Sorry, Mr M. The matter's closed. We could never invite you anywhere again should the question of cost raise its ugly head.'

Standing to acknowledge their generosity, I hit my head upon the rack.

After classes next day, a meeting between Olive Brownlow, a groggy Fay Passmore and myself was called in the Café de l'Université opposite the Fac.

Miss Brownlow came straight to the point.

'I have to admit it, Mr M. My French isn't quite up to what's being required of me.'

'Nonsense, Miss Brownlow!'

'Oh I do wish you'd drop that "Miss" and call me Olive!'

'What will you have to drink, ladies?'

'Whatever you recommend.'

'Two panachés and a blanc cassis.'

The waitress has cherry lips. A silver cross escapes from her cleavage as though the excitement of intimacy within has been too hard to bear in darkness and in solitude. The purse beneath her frilly apron bulges where the womb would swell if she bore my child. Would she were younger and I could manage her! Her eyes stare insolently at mine. It is more than I can do to place the order without trembling.

'Such a pretty girl!' says Miss Passmore. 'Too much eye-shadow, but nevertheless very pretty.'

Miss Brownlow shrugs her ample shoulders:

'Two a penny. By the way, Mr M., what's a panaché? You must teach us everything you can. We're in your hands.'

'A . . .'

Miss Passmore interrupts her.

'Tell Mr Mildew, Olive, what you want of him.'

Mr M., I wonder would you draft my letter of thanks to our hosts yesterday at Amancey?'

She catches my flicker of resistance.

'There, Fay! I told you he'd consider it an imposition!'

'Sssh, Olive!'

'Fay, pass me the bill. I want it in easy reach.'

'Allow me!' I interpose.

'Certainly not! It was we who dragged you here. You wouldn't entertain two has-beens like us of your own volition!'

I draft their letter.

One further point arises: should one tip the coach driver?

'A matter for conscience, head and heart, ladies. If he has been helpful, or if you wish he were more helpful in the days to come. If he has been efficient, or if you wish he were more efficient . . .'

'But how much do you suggest?' Miss Brownlow labours.

'Fifty centimes from each of the party would be more than adequate.'

'I'll ask for thirty, then . . . And what about the student guide?'

'Nothing!'

I visited the piscine one morning when I thought the Ladies were supposed to be at classes. To my horror, five were spluttering and floundering there, setting up tidal waves of ultra-marine which negated the tranquillity I anticipated. I had darted down some steps, and placed myself nimbly beside an innocent on the cement terrace bordering the river. Her eyes were closed. She would not be afraid. A drop of perspiration coursed down the slopes of her smooth, curvaceous thigh. I yearned to finger her dimpled land-scape.

'Look who's here! So you've finally caught us! Teachers skipping classes!'

It was that nuisance, Wendolyn Moxey.

The girl I had been venerating sat up, adjusting the straps of her bikini. A lorry thundered over the Pont Bregille in a cloud of dust. The cathedral bell clanked out the hour.

'Time, I'm afraid, to get back to work at the library.'

She was not convinced.

'Oh dear, I've disturbed you. Boys will be boys and I've gone and spoiled everything! I always forget men must have their moments on their own!' She winked knowingly. The girl had got up and left. '. . . We'll be seeing you on Saturday's excursion, won't we? The coach leaves from the front of the Cité at eight o'clock. It's the Haut Doubs this time . . . But Olive will have told you . . .' Why this excitement? Why this spate of words? Was she in love with me? I was puzzled. 'Till Saturday, then, Mr Mildew! Au revoir!'

No man is an island—least of all in my predicament. One minute past the hour, and I was standing with the Ladies who, shielding their eyes, peered anxiously into the morning haze for a coach that had not arrived. Mule-like they staggered under the uneven weights of plastic macks and umbrellas, and brief-cases, rucksacks and bags crammed with maps, casse-croûtes, aspirins, sticking plaster, fly repellent, cameras, dictionaries, Fox's Glacier Mints and sugar barley.

'Let's not tip him for being late like this!' suggests Miss Farley of Bath indignantly.

'Shame!' and 'Have a heart!' is heard from the Outer Pale.

'Maybe he's had an accident,' I venture. 'Maybe he's dead.'

'For so mild looking a fellow, Mr M., you're very morbid!'

'You know,' I hear Mrs Slatter say behind her hand to Miss Jones, 'there's something about that Mildew man I'm not quite sure of. He goes to the cupboard to blow his nose.'

'Let's not beat about the bush, Sally. The man's furtive!'

Fay Passmore sees I have overheard and blushes, I imagine, beneath her lizardy tan:

54

'Yes, very sportif.'

'Sportif?' Miss Jones looks astonished.

Miss Passmore ventriloquises that I have been listening.

'Blood and sand!'

'Oh Lord!'

Now *they* look furtive!

So Miss Passmore is an ally. I shall call her Fay.

Miss Farley addresses me:

'It's *so* caned of you to take another day off to accompany us Ladies in Distress!'

'Spoiled for choice, aren't you?' interferes Miss Westbright of South Ken.

'Indeed I am!' I concur enthusiastically.

'Oh will this stupid bus never arrive!'

The group, excepting its leader, raises a united wail of pained sympathy. 'Let's hope this weather will hold!' she says irrelevantly, then adds, 'Aren't those reflections in the water beautiful!'

Those that bend over the wall of the quayside to check this observation soon straighten up again. They realize they have been cheated. 'Olive has been applying one of her psychological tricks to put our minds at rest,' complains Miss Jones.

Eyes are now trained upon a coach on the Pont Battant. Will it turn left towards us, or drive straight on? Knuckles whiten. Will it, won't it? Is it ours, isn't it? Yes! No! Yes!! Handkerchieves, brollies and scarves are waved excitedly. Someone screams.

I fear that the students sleeping off their latest revelries in the Cité may be wakened. That would never do. They might be rendered too fatigued to hold another of their demonstrations in the Place St Pierre or to debate in the Amphi Donzelot of the Fac the latest nonsense being staged in Paris.

'Ladies, ladies! Please!!' laughs Olive Brownlow uncomfortably. 'Remember we are ambassadresses!' She turns to me. 'Well, *that's* a worry off my mind. I thought he'd *never* come.'

Since when has punctuality been a French characteristic? The remark emphasises her inexperience.

All aboard. It's a heave for most—a chance to prove agility for the athletic Fay. The driver sits glumly at his wheel awaiting our student guide.

To Miss Westbright's disappointment, it is the actress who

appropriates me first this morning. A piece of cigarette smoke catches in the latter's gullet. She chokes and sways to great effect.

'Come and nurse an invalid! Should I die in the course of today's journey, my fortune shall be yours!'

The coughing alters to convulsive merriment at such a notion. I move to be alone.

The word goes round.

'Sarah Bernhardt's upset Mr Mildew!'

'Mr Mildew's in a huff!'

'Trust her!'

'Trust him, you mean!'

Soon, though, the dust settles. Each has freshened up with a quick dab of this and that, checked her smile, waggled a finger to a friend, pulled her skirt smooth—and the student guide, who has reached us unshaven, decides to meet respectability half way, and combs his hair. We are ready to set off.

'Mesdames, Mesdemoiselles, Monsieur—bonjour! The only alteration to the splendid trip ahead of us as printed on your programmes culturels is that we shall not be visiting the Château de Joux . . .'

Incomprehension on the part of the Ladies.

'I repeat that we shall *not* be visiting the Château de Joux . . . Nevertheless I trust you will find our time together happy and instructive. Bonne journée!' He makes an exaggerated bow and jokes with the driver. The Ladies clap.

We arrive at Ornans too early to visit the museum.

The Jura amounts to no more than uniform valleys and out-crops of rocky tedium.

In the Loue Valley, the Ladies' high-pitched voices frighten the fish.

We peep over the edge of a ravine, then descend by bumpy narrow roads past wood-stacks and cowslip verges to Pontarlier.

The radio blares:

> Congratulations
> And celebrations
> When I tell ev'ryone that you're in love with me
> Congratulations
> And jubilations
> I want the world to know I'm happy as can be.

Would that I could respond in the mood of the lyric to Miss Moxey and Miss Westbright's advances!

'Half an hour, Ladies and Gentleman!'

A schoolmaster has mounted a show of wooden shoes, fans, kimonos, hand-painted flowers and other japonaiserie in a disused chapel in the main street.

Waiting for the guide and driver, I ask Wendolyn Moxey has she seen the exhibition.

'So you've decided to speak to me at last! All hoity-toity we were this morning, moving away from me as if I had BO!'

I repeat my question.

'*Japanese* exhibition in Pontarlier! You must be *joking*! Pull the other one, Mr Mildew!'

'It was rather fun. A secondary schoolmaster arranged it. You'd still have time if you went quickly. It's along there, in the old Chapelle des Annonciades.'

'In a chapel?!' Miss Farley is horrified.

Others consider it their duty to support her:

'I'm not a believer but . . .'

'Rather unusual, to put it mildly!'

Miss Farley presses her point home:

'My brother served in Burma. You can have no idea of what he saw and suffered.'

'A slap in the face to your brother!'

'A slap in the face to God, you mean!'

'I'm with you there, Alice, one hundred per cent!'

'Dear oh dear, ladies! In drawing your attention to what I thought was rather an enterprising effort by a member of your own profession, I'd no idea I was stirring a hornet's nest!'

They are soon eating humble pie again because they want advice. Mrs Slatter asks me to estimate the duty on a watch she has bought for one of her four fine sons. When, eventually, we re-board, Miss Moxey touches the seat beside her as I pass.

'Where next?' She consults her programme. 'Montbenoit Abbey, followed by lunch at Villers-le-Lac and a walk by the Roche du Prêtre.'

The Abbey is bitterly cold. Workmen hammer in the roof. A cleaner hoovers a carpet in front of the altar.

We drive past dandelion meadows to Villers-le-Lac.

I join the Inner Circle on the windy terrace of the Hôtel de l'Union. I advise them they will not be welcome unles they buy some wine. They suggest ordinaire. I order Beaujolais.

The Ladies unpack their casse-croûtes while the guide and driver eat sumptuously in the interior.

'Tuck in, Mr M.!'

'Yes, help yourself!'

'The tomatoes cost only 3.30 a kilo at Besançon market!'

The waitress is hovering. I pay her ten francs for our wine and collect fourteen from the Ladies.

'Thank heavens we've Mr Mildew!'

'Have an apple, but don't forget to wipe it first!'

Half way between here and the next attraction, Miss Brownlow produces sheaves of song sheets.

'Let's beat them at their own game and sing their Godforsaken radio out of business!'

We do her bidding.

'She goes, poor thing, to so much trouble!' titters Wendy Moxey.

The bombast of 'Auprès de ma Blonde' gives way to a maudlin version of 'Poor Old Joe':

> Me voilà, me voilà
> Tout brisé par les travaux
> J'entends leurs douces voix chanter
> 'Hého Vieux Joe.'

The guide raises a hand as we are launching into the second verse.

'Ladies and Gentleman! Much as I regret interrupting such charming choralists—charming to behold and charming to hear . . .' He winks at the driver and lights a cigar. 'Delightful as your singing was, no is . . .' He draws in the smoke with juvenile pomposity.

'Get on with it! Get on with it!' Miss Moxey is provoked. She drums her fingers against the seat in front.

'. . . I must tell you something of the beauty spot at which we are about to halt . . .'

He pauses mid-speech to mould a smoke-ring.

'This is too much!'

'Sssh, Olive! He may hear you!' reproves Fay.

'Frankly I don't care if he does!'

'. . . The Roche du Prêtre dominates a view of savage splend-our, unsurpassed in the region, unsurpassed, indeed, in any region you may care to mention . . .'

He drank too much wine at lunch.

'. . . The rock owes its name to the fact that a priest fell to his death one stormy night, bringing succour to a member of his parish. Should any amongst you wish to depart this life by the same method, do not hesitate to take advantage of this unparal-lelled opportunity!'

He guffaws childishly. The driver apes him, seduced by some-one he mistakenly considers his superior.

The Ladies are uncomfortable. The guide spoke thickly, but at a speed which enabled them to grasp that they were being twitted.

We alight.

'Mucky brutes!'

Mrs Slatter has stepped onto a cow-pat.

What would she have said had she tasted the faecal currants concealed in my food by ill-wishers at Hurdleford Jail?

4

Sunday, 12th May

The students, workers' sons for the most part, have had the audacity to strike in protest against their Napoleonic legacy. Their fathers plan a General Strike tomorrow. The Post Office has ceased to operate already: the Ladies, whose cours de perfectionnement is to continue come what may, weep for lack of news from dear ones.

My Editor has recommended that I use the smouldering situation to my own advantage. The suggestion is preposterous, but typical of Grub Street. I have better things to do than root around the student hang-outs for a story.

This afternoon, no stranger to my hopefulness could have guessed the urges throbbing through my veins as I sat on the Veil-Picard quayside watching contestants prepare for a canoe race. One girl wore rubbery trunks and a woollen jersey which moulded her North and South with perfect candour. After indulging in playful antics with her rivals, she was persuaded to do a trial run. Midstream the current conquered her. Her canoe capsized. A redhead rescued her. He dried her with a towel and walked with arm about her to a dormobile. This is what I seek! To serve, to touch, to comfort—though not, like he, to ravish. Have no fear, my pretty ones! No need to flee from me across the brow of Chaudanne! The via media is my rule. Which is why, much as I dislike the police, I remain neutral in the present conflict.

Each faction is repugnant to me.

The students avail themselves of their free time, not to study, but to march, make public speeches and shout at one another in mindless debate. They loathe Parisians, yet they affect to emulate the violence of their 'camarades' in the vicinity of St Germain-des-Près. Pickets are stationed outside the Fac des Lettres and, further out of town, the Fac des Sciences. I wonder how the Purple Warrior, anxious to benefit his fellow-negroes in Malawi, takes this costly interruption.

On Tuesday last, demonstrators marched before the Hôtel de Police. Their banners read 'End Repression!' and 'Liberty of Expression for the Unions!' Unopposed, they dispersed at the Préfecture.

On Wednesday, a contingent chanted 'Ouvriers avec Nous!' and 'Libérez Nos Camarades!' in the Grande Rue, while a police Peugeot politely followed after.

That morning, Olive Brownlow contacted me at the Municipal Library where, under the marble-cool busts of Cuvier and the Abbé Boisot, I was comparing the rue Pasteur tourelle in Coindre's 'Mon Vieux Besançon' with those of Old Scotland Yard. Poor Miss Brownlow! She had decamped from a conducted tour of the Centre Regional de Documentation Pédagogique because the Directeur had informed her that, to wind off the proceedings, his staff wished to join the Ladies in a vin d'honneur to celebrate the ending of hostilities against the Germans.

'It's in a quarter of an hour!' She was quite breathless.

'Believe me, there is nothing more moving than sincere sentiments expressed with difficulty in a foreign tongue.'

'I'm not sincere. I mean . . . What I mean is the French were no damned use to us in the war, were they?'

I agreed to help her.

I spoke of Our Two Great Nations, of Our Norman Heritage, of how, as a seafaring Welfare State, we had benefited from Besançon's two illustrious sons, the Marquis de Jouffroy d' Abbans, inventor of the steamship, and Proudhon, inventor of the social conscience; I raised my glass to the future prosperity of France and to her continuing example in the world—on a day when the activities of the young in Paris, and to a lesser extent in Besançon, resembled the squeals of Hitler Youth in the nineteen-thirties!

Is there anywhere in Europe, I ask myself, that is free from the present turmoil? Order has been threatened in Rome, Milan, Brussels, Oslo and Berlin. It seems that, on the rim of these wheels also, the simple-minded have been inveigled by a handful of hooligans into disgracing themselves.

Here in Besançon, I must eat in the same building, share the same table with provocateurs. One is met at the restaurant gates by uncouth extremists who press upon one leaflets which their equally uncouth readers scan with nodding sympathy, then chuck upon the pathways. The outside of the canteen is chequered with white, yellow and green papers issuing from the CFDT, CGT, FO, FEN, SNESup, SGEN and the AGEB-UNEF, initials no doubt meaningful to the gum-chewing boors who distribute and discard them. Students, workers, all of us, are asked to unite in order to attain democratic liberty and the right to free expression which, no doubt, includes the right to strew the ground with rubbish—and to queue-dodge. On one occasion I found as many as ten newcomers between myself and those behind whom I was originally standing. I buttonholed one of them.

'Young man, is your "movement", as you call it, in the cause of justice and a new morality?'

'Most certainly it is, comrade!'

'Then take your place in the line!'

He and his friends laughed loudly at what they considered to be my splendid sense of humour.

I cannot fathom why the authorities are feeding them at all. Why not shut them out? They're not decent, hardworking individuals with a grievance like myself. They're a horde of sexual degenerates. Morning, afternoon and evening, when they are not canvassing for political support, they lounge and loll in public places in an expression of what they deem to be 'universal love'. La liberté d'aimer! One expects them to sink to the ground and fornicate at one's feet 'in protest'. In protest against what? Against the public's right to an absence of nauseating exhibitionism?'

Fortunately I have at last found myself a supreme distraction from this sickening brew of undergraduate delinquency. I thought I had been doomed to dally on this Earth, a feckless Orpheus without his Proserpine. But no!

I returned one lunchtime to the long grasses by the Ecole de Ponts, hoping to witness soldiers and their girlfriends discreetly courting by the water. I was thinking happily that the police would now be too occupied to concern themselves with spying on me and my kind, and that I might, while the revolution continued, relax my prudence. All at once I thought I saw a képi jutting from the undergrowth.

With heart pounding, I walked away and, as I did so, a girl, her skirts flying, rode past me on a bicycle into the Gare d'Eau. I strolled after her with studied unconcern. Was I being watched? Best bluff it out, I thought. Maybe the girl had parked her machine to linger in the sunlight like myself. No law could prevent me from judiciously pursuing her.

But, turning the corner, I found that she had vanished. The waters of the harbour mirrored my fear and disappointment. Beneath the slime, alongside moored vedettes, sinister carp, like great grey submarines, glided among a myriad of translucent-bellied bleak. Uneasily I retraced my steps and crossed the willowed bridge to the towpath which leads to the Citadelle's escarpment.

Here was a prettier sight—rows of lettuce and young peas; rhubarb, strawberries and chives. A woman, two toddlers romping round her in knickers and wide hats, was weeding the sandy soil at her allotment gate where bloomed a fine display of clustered pinks.

I struck up conversation.

'Perfect soil for pinks.'

She looked up, startled.

'What?'

'Perfect soil for pinks. Nice and sandy.'

'I suppose so.'

My body stiffened: an agent de police was walking along the towpath towards us.

'We've met before,' I stammered, attempting to extend our talk and hide my face from the enemy approaching.

'Have we? When? Forgive me! Are you a shopkeeper here?'

'You flatter me. I'm not entirely French.'

'I don't believe you. Somewhere from the south, surely! I know. We met in Marseille last year!'

'Not Marseille, I do assure you!'

'Where then?'

The policeman was level. He stopped. He placed his hand on the allotment gate. I panicked. I prepared to make a dash for it.

'Marcel! Meet Monsieur . . .'

'Ploedic,' I extemporized.

'Monsieur Ploedic, my husband Marcel Eliasar. Monsieur Ploedic says he knows me, Marcel!'

'I have passed Madame and her children in this garden so often that I feel I know her.'

'Ah!' She wiped her forehead with the back of her hand.

'How fortunate, Monsieur, to preside over such an attractive family!'

'Monsieur is too kind!'

'One question. Are your pinks always so quick to bloom? The second week in May seems . . .'

'It was the March sunshine that helped. Allow me to pick you some.'

And this from one of the breed that has so long oppressed me!

'There, Monsieur! With the compliments of the season!'

I was touched, then tempted to hurl them in the water.

Common sense prevailed:

'Thank you! How very kind! And now I must be on my way! Delighted . . . Au revoir!'

Curbing my instinct to break into a cowardly sprint, I turned to wave at intervals for the next fifty yards.

Suddenly the pinks were knocked from my hand.

'Watch where you're going! . . . Oh, I do apologize!' I was face to face with one of André Planson's nymphs beside the Marne. 'My fault! My fault entirely! I had my back to you!'

My gaze was drawn towards her domey buttocks as she stooped to gather up my flowers.

'Who's the lucky lady?' Handing them back, she winked broadly.

'Lady? Oh! I see your meaning! No lady in particular.'

She pouted her lips. '*I'm* a lady.'

'So I perceive! Very much so!'

'Well then?'

'Well then what?'

'You could give them to *me*.'

'But of course! I didn't think that after they'd fallen . . .'

'Why so bashful?'

I presented them at once. She expressed her pleasure:

'Wish there were more like you about! Life's a bit dull round here. Why not let's meet again some time!'

'Yes, yes! Any time! When, my dear? Tonight?'

'Monday. The Promenade Charlotte. Ten o'clock. Bye-bye for now!'

'Don't go!'

'Sorry! We open again at two.'

'We?'

'The Bon Marché.'

'You work there? Let me accompany you!'

'No need. We agreed Monday, remember?'

'I don't know your name!'

Too late. I was left alone to marvel at Life's mystery, the swiftness of Her acts of bounty as well as of Her cruelties.

Nor was it illusion. She *does* work at the Bon Marché. I have seen her since, moving like quicksilver at her employer's bidding. I have seen her subtly signal me as she pinned a sale's notice to a riot of rough towelling in the window. I have seen her place a brassière against her breasts to entertain me before laying it on a trellissed arch among its sisters.

Till Monday! Till tomorrow, darling! I shall not, meanwhile, disclose our secret, except among these pages.

> J'ai eu longtemps un visage inutile
> Mais maintenant
> J'ai un visage pour être aimé
> J'ai un visage pour être heureux!

In you I place my hopes, my sweet! It is you whom I appoint to liberate the harassed chambers of my brain! For too many years have I stood before my looking-glass, weeping at the spectre that I see reflected there, and wishing I were truly wicked. It is my good intentions which have undone me, deprived me of the privilege of a guilty conscience. Have I been too strong in not insisting on compliance? Should I, this time, darling, take you selfishly, irrespective of your own desires? Should I, in exchange for a lifetime's abstinence, offer society the depravity it expects?

Has this dallying, this caution, been a contrived routine of self-deception? Have I, in failing to exercise my member, diminished its potency? Have I spared each of my pretty ones, not for a greater and more glorious state of virtue, but for the likes of the barbarians who now threaten the framework of civilized existence?

No more procrastination! With the makeshift armour of my learning, with the lance that has not been tried, with only the Pole Star of my sensibility to guide me, I shall ride into battle, brooking no obstruction. Never fear, my unspoilt Princess of the Doubs and of the Bon Marché! I have heard your cries for help. I shall be within reach of you by tomorrow night in the Promenade Charlotte, where I shall lead a different revolution from the rest, where I shall kiss the lips the law forbids me kiss, where I, too, shall demand la liberté d'aimer, but in another style.

Sweet Bisontine! You are the chosen instrument of my completion! Annie, my astral guide, has led me to you, held out her hand across the abyss of time to aid me. I shall kneel at your feet in humble bondage. The fruit which was taken from me has now ripened.

5

Tuesday, 28th May

La Belle France is at a standstill. Pseudo-intellectualism has corrupted the workers. There has been shooting in the market place. Factories, banks and schools are closed. The Bibliothèque Municipale is closed : I must use the Bibliothèque de l'Université at the discretion of the students I detest. That able physician, the Général de Gaulle, will have to diagnose and prescribe quickly. The Ladies only continue with their studies on the basis of a technicality, namely that the Centre de Linguistique Appliquée which devised their course is not state-subsidized. Suppliers of gas and electricity, and, to the relief of the Ladies, the hair-dressers, continue to fulfil their duties. So does the staff of the Bon Marché.

I arrived at the rendezvous with my dear one in the Promenade Charlotte a little early. I was trespassing on yet another Fairies' hunting ground. They wriggled and gesticulated in malicious concert. They jingled their bracelets in undisguised impatience at my presence.

'Tu cherches une bitte?'

'. . . un trou?'

I ignored their crudities.

'Oh là là! So debonair!'

'So special!'

'So unattainable!'

I remained aloof. Believing I was condemning their nature and not their manner, they resorted like students to abuse :

'Hypocrite!'

'Snob!'

I felt bound to protest :

'Inaccurate and most unfair!'

Only the arrival of my sweetheart saved me. They scattered when I spoke to her.

'I was terrified!'

'Of *them*!' she laughed. 'At least they are young and pretty!'

'And *I* am not?'

'Never mind!'

She dragged me affectionately into the deepest shadows.

I was alarmed by her insouciance. She was over-attracted by me. In her eagerness, she forgot the inaptness of our whereabouts, and demanded more than kisses.

Old habits die hard. The gravity of my responsibility over-whelmed me. I pinioned to her sides the hands that strayed so fretfully. I raised my chin to disengage her agitated lips. She, in response, ran her cheek against my chest and, pushing me against the stonework of the statue of La Charlotte, pressed her thighs to mine till it seemed her silky skirt no longer kept me from her nakedness.

'No, my dear! No, you mustn't!'

'Why? Why?'

'We must get to know each other.'

'We already know each other. What are we waiting for?'

'Standing here!'

'Where else, then?'

'Nowhere!'

I was ashamed of my room's simplicity, its bachelor untidiness, my socks hanging on the unscoured bidet.

'*No*where?'

'Not tonight.'

'Tonight or never!' . . .

Thus we haggled.

Her petulance entranced me.

'My darling!'

'Why call me "darling"? You won't *do* anything!'

I explained myself:

'I must see your parents. They must approve.'

'Of what?'

'Of us. Of my interest in you. We must tell them how we met.'

'*Exactly* how we met?'

'Well, not *exactly*!'

'You could be a salesman at the shop! A fabric salesman.'

'Fabricatrice!'

'Oh, you're so clever and so funny! I adore you!'

Her hands were working at my buttons.

'You must be getting home.'

'I can't. Beure's too far to walk.'

'Why not take a bus?'

'There's the Strike, silly!'

'How did you get here, then?'

'My brother drove me in his car. He's at a student meeting.'

'Let him drive you back! . . .' But this was selfish. 'Oh, all right! I'll pay for a taxi!'

She softened in the security of my kindliness.

'You be good to me and I'll be good to you!'

'But I don't even know your name, my dear!'

'Lucienne.'

'Lucienne "who"?'

'Just Lucienne.'

'Your *sur*name, child!'

'Farouchette. Lucienne Farouchette.'

'Delightful! My name is Toby Mildew.'

She repeated it—and incorrectly. I found the attempt fetching.

'Jolly well done, Lucienne! Jolly well done!'

She asked me to take her to a café with a télé juke-box. We sat in a darkened corner.

I crossed the room and inserted a coin at her request. I turned to look at her. She seemed, in her nook, so helplessly alluring. Thank God I hadn't taken advantage of her desperate forwardness to break her crystal vase. I must induct her reverently.

'Another coffee?'

'Sssh! I want to hear the music.'

The performer, a swarthy Mexican, appeared to sing as he leaped from a fence onto a covered wagon.

The picture flickered out. Lucienne remained hypnotized.

'It's over,' I reminded her.

'Well then, put me on another!'

'By the way, I've bought you a present.'

'Present!'

She tore at the wrapping excitedly.

'I hope it will be the first of many.'

69

'A lucky charm! Oh thank you! Thank you! How kind!'
She kissed me on both cheeks. 'You dear old man! I love you!'
' "Love!" That word is sacred!'
'I mean it! I mean it! Promise not to leave me ever!'
We drifted out beneath the stars to find a taxi.
I pointed to a caryatid near the Square St Amour.
'Beautiful, isn't it?'
'Will you take me to the Ascension Day Fair?'
'But that's too far ahead!'
'I've got the whole day off. Of course, if you don't want to . . .'
'You know I want to. Where shall we meet?'
'The bus stop opposite the Gare Viotte.'
'What time?'
'Two-thirty. Got ten francs?'
'Ten francs?'
'My fare home.'
I owed the patron one week's rent, but, for fear of losing her,
I paid her readily.

It would have been an imposture at such a juncture to deny
we were all animals. Some of us, though, were more animal than
others. The students, for instance, had already desecrated the
town and university. The red flag of Communism flew beside
the black of Anarchy outside the Faculté des Lettres. On the
wall of the staircase to the library was scribbled 'The strike is
spreading. The factories are occupied—Renault, Nantes, St
Nazaire, Sud Aviation'. On another wall I read 'All united for
a university that is free and for the people'.

It appalled me that so many of the university staff, including
Professor Godon, continued to support the students. Didn't Louis
XVI only love his people till he was certain his head was to be
removed! College canteens remained open to the rebels. Special
billboards were placed at their disposal. They were still allowed
to distribute propaganda leaflets seething with incitement and
sedition and often contradicting the spirit of their headlines—
'We must emerge from chaos', 'Jesus said unto him, Go and do
thou likewise', 'We respect the freedom to work'. Yes, you res-
pected the freedom to work, yet labelled those who try to instruct
the Ladies as black-legs. The same ladies were frightened out of
their wits by your antics! Why else would the stout-hearted Miss

Brownlow and Miss Passmore have packed their bags in hopes of being flown back home by mercy mission? Is there any wonder that hysteria was rife when in blood red on a wall of the rue Mégevand was daubed the words, 'DE GAULLE ASSASSIN', and when 'CON' was chalked foully on the Post Office to be seen by decent citizens?!

On Ascension Day, I waited for Lucienne as pre-arranged. A private firm had organized a shuttle coach service between the Gare Viotte and the Fair at Planoise so as not to disappoint the crowds.

I watched her climb the hill. She was wearing an orange blouse and a white accordion-pleated skirt. She swung her handbag with such innocent abandon that the other holiday-makers, judging from their smiles, experienced as much exhilaration from watching her as I did.

I waved. Though recognizing me, she did not answer.

'Lucienne, my dear! I was so afraid that after yesterday it would rain again today!'

'Couldn't care less!'

Raised eyebrows. Quizzical smirks from bystanders. I identified one of the Micaud-Charlotte Fairies. His shoulders twitched in disdainful amusement.

So Lucienne was ahead of me! She had been embarrassed. She had observed already that the bus-queue was querying our connection.

'We have to stare this out, dear, whatever people think.'

'I've no idea what you're talking about!'

'Do I disappoint you? I realize I'm no Yves Montand.'

'Your suit!'

'What's wrong with my suit?'

'A waistcoat on a day like this!'

'I *beg* your pardon!'

'And your panama's ridiculous!'

I thought of Portia's description of herself to Bassanio in 'The Merchant of Venice':

'. . . . an unlesson'd girl, unschool'd, unpractis'd:
Happy in this, she is not yet so old
But she may learn . . .'

71

'My dear, *I'll* be the judge of fashion. Besides, formality may prove to your advantage when I take you to smart places!'

She picked an imaginary speck of dust from my lapel, and smiled. Jammed tight inside the bus, she fondled me.

The Ladies would have envied her.

Miss Patsy Jones had to lecture to the group some weeks ago in front of an instructor—her subject: 'Painting—The Modern Movement'. She confided to me that her ignorance of Art matched her ignorance of the French language. 'Frankly,' she said, 'I don't know a Van Gogh from a Van Heusen!'

I produced an essay. She was effusive in her thanks.

She approached me diffidently a week later.

'I need slides from the Centre Pédagogique to use as illustrations. The building has been closed. Would you, I implore you, plead with the Occupying Committee on my behalf?'

I did so. I referred to the accepted codes of hospitality towards defenceless women in a foreign land, and to the imperilling of international relations. I obtained the slides.

'How, oh how can I ever repay you, Mr Mildew!'

'I would tell you if I were not afraid of losing stature in your eyes.'

'Impossible to lose stature after this!'

'Expected funds from London haven't reached me . . .'

'If it's money you are short of, name the amount and you shall have it!'

'The matter won't go any further?'

'How much do you want?'

'Twenty francs.'

'Twenty!! Here's fifty!'

'But that's far too much! The banks will be closing! You'll need every sou!'

'Here you are, and not another word!'

Miss Farley of Bath was talking on Local Pottery. Because the Institut d'Archéologie is closed, she invited me to tea at La Viennoise, away from her rivals at the Décombe, in order to pick my brains.

'What is a "poinçon"? . . . And what exactly is a "vase à coup de poing"?'

The information was worth another fifty francs.

The Banque de France closed down on the 20th, at two o'clock.

I found Miss Westbright next morning by the Place Granvelle peering beseechingly through glass doors at clerks playing with toy cars and trucks. She knocked in vain. I hurried to assist her. One of the idlers reluctantly came out to us, supplied the name of a branch that was still conducting business.

Sixty francs.

I was now sufficiently in funds to satisfy my angel's whims—taxis, the télé juke-box, yet another present at the Fair today . . .

The 'Train Texas' was yellow and red, motor-driven and with open carriages. Around the grounds we rode like a couple on a Blackpool outing. Lucienne tapped her feet. She waved. What a transformation from my sullen companion after lunch! I allowed her impulses to lead me where they willed. Entering into the spirit of the festival, I shared her enthusiasm for activities which, under other conditions, I would have considered trite.

She took me to stalls of local products—rye bread, cherrywood wardrobes, ugly bahuts bas. She tried a Singer sewing-machine. She tatted at the stand of Tapis Mod. Wide-eyed she ran to watch a chef make crêpes flambées . . .

I could hardly keep pace.

'Your hand shakes!' she told me at the rifle range.

'You look worn out!' she giggled as we climbed from a rocket roundabout.

On a dodgem, she bumped us till I felt unwell.

I bought her twenty raffle tickets which she eagerly unscrewed. 'I've won! I've won!' she cried, and dappled me with promises of later favours.

She chose a Bambi with an orange bow which matched her blouse.

I bought her a strawberry tart, then some Japanese pearls in the Hall of Trade.

'You're so good to me, Toby!'

'Will you always let me be good to you?'

'Always! Always!'

Leaving the grounds, I saw the Purple Warrior buying a toffee-apple for a Fairy. He saw me with Lucienne. We understood one another, made immediate allowances and did not intrude. The more negros the merrier, say I.

We dined on the Chaland boat. On our way there through the

C*   73

Promenade Micaud Lucienne asked me to explain its 'funny pillars'.

'Those "funny pillars" as you call them are a Tuscan Folly, an ornamental ruin.'

I was pleased that she showed interest in something beyond herself. The educational process was beginning.

But she didn't yet know that one may use one's fingers to remove a fishbone from the mouth. And when I asked her which wine she preferred—Arbois or Château-Chalon—she looked completely blank. There is much ground to cover before I dare present her in London. Madame Prunier would give her a rueful eye.

'Like a piece of gum?' she invited during coffee.

'With coffee ! !'

'The peppermint flavour goes nicely,' she explained.

I was sorry I'd rebuffed her. After all, she had still so little to give me save her body.

'Thank you and I'll have it later . . . You bring me much happiness, Lucienne!'

'And you've given me my lucky charm, my Japanese pearls and Bambi! You must come to meet my family on Sunday. Maman is terribly excited.'

'About meeting me?'

'No, stupid! It's Mothers' Day. It was postponed this year because of the Revolution. Don't you know anything?'

'Isn't it time I put you in a taxi to go home?'

'I want you to take me back with you tonight.'

Though I was apprehensive, the temptation was too great.

'You'll hate my room,' I warned her as I turned the key.

'Oh I'm sure I've been in worse places. Has it a bed?'

'Sssh!'

I locked the door on the other side. She put her bag and Bambi on the table, and began unbuttoning her blouse.

'Wait till I draw the curtains!' I whispered. 'The patron!'

'He's normal, isn't he?'

I allowed her to undress.

She lay down on the bed.

'Play with me!'

'Please not so loud, Lucienne! The walls are paper thin.'

'Men bring women to hotel rooms, don't they?'

74

'Women—not girls!'

She sat up angrily. 'I don't excite you?'

I tried to calm her with a kiss. I almost wished she were some-what afraid of me, like the Annie I remembered.

'Aren't you ever going to undress?' she persisted.

'Your parents! If they found out, what would they think of me?!'

'This is 1968!'

'I can't bring myself to do it!'

' Not even on Ascension Day?'

I was astounded by the sophistication of the pun, coming as it did from a mere midinette.

'I've a good mind to spank you for that!'

'You try!'

I did so. She gave a girlish scream and, as I stifled it, bit my thumb.

'Petit chameau!' I jumped off the bed. 'This has gone far enough! Get dressed!'

'But you haven't even kissed me!'

'Yes, I have!'

'Call that a real kiss?'

She was pretending to be more worldly than in fact she could be. No girl who was not an innocent would take such risks with a stranger in a hotel bedroom.

'I said "Get dressed"!'

'Come here!'

Refusing to budge, she stretched out her arms towards me.

'No! You must give me time! My heart aches for you, but you must give me time!'

'Tomorrow? You'll be better tomorrow?'

'Yes, tomorrow! Visit me tomorrow!'

'You promise to be more friendly?'

'Promise!'

She rolled off the bed.

'Help me up, Toby! This linoleum's cold.'

She tried to drag me down as I stooped to do her bidding. I only escaped her grasp by slipping from my jacket.

She stood up crossly.

'I want to do pipi, don't you?'

She arranged herself upon the bidet.

'Wait!' I said and, while I fumbled to remove my socks which were drying there, she slid back so that I could do pipi also.

Our act of sharing was moving in its simplicity.

Afterwards, I helped her into her garments one by one.

'Tomorrow?'

'Tomorrow,' she answered, picking up her Bambi and checking that her pearls were secure.

'You sound tired, my love. I'll come with you to the taxi.'

'Don't bother.'

'Don't bother!! It's unthinkable you walk the streets alone!'

'My brother will have parked his car in the rue Lacore.'

'I wasn't aware there was a debate tonight.'

'He's gone to see *My Fair Lady*.'

'Why park, then, in the rue Lacore? The cinema's nowhere near it! Look, dearest, I see you wish to spare me trouble, but, don't you understand, I *want* your company!'

'Give me the taxi money now! I don't want to appear cheap in front of the driver.'

'I thought you said you were going home in your brother's car.'

'I've changed my mind. The film won't be over for an hour. As you said, I mustn't walk the streets alone. Please let me take a taxi!'

I gave her ten francs. She tried the door.

'You locked it!'

'Of course I locked it!'

'I was your prisoner and you did nothing!'

I embraced her.

The next evening, she brought me her mother's 1933 edition of *Sans Famille* by Victor Malot. Could any gift have been more apposite? I read her a chapter. Interspersed among the pages were the sweetest little feminine things—viola and narcissus leaves, cologne and scent labels, a plastic hen. I sleep with them beneath my pillow.

I had bought her a Ludo set, to keep her mind off naughtier things. From the impatient way she threw the dice, I thought she might retract the invitation to meet her parents. No—on Mothers' Day, her car-driving brother, Georges, as prepossessing as the Phantom of the Rue Morgue, arrived to collect me, and, armed with Réserve de l'Empereur for Monsieur and the traditional box of liqueur cherries for Madame, I was put down, shortly after midday, at the family bungalow in Beure.

Monsieur and Madame were waiting respectfully in the porch to greet me. They accepted their gifts with such fitting meekness that I was tempted to shed the disguise of salesman and inform them of my profession—until I reached the living-room where not a single book stood on the shelves. In accepting *Sans Famille*, I had robbed the Farouchettes of their literary heritage.

Monsieur introduced me proudly to two more sons and an infant daughter.

'Guy is reading Chemistry and Biology.'

He was pale and unsmiling—one of the faceless planners who will one day dictate to us the functions of our genital organs.

'I didn't realize students permitted themselves to read anything at the present time!'

'Now, now! No politics today, Monsieur Milledieu! We don't want Guy and Georges at one another's throat! Georges, who's studying Philosophie at the Fac des Lettres, is particularly militant. Ah, here he is! Georges, I'm introducing Monsieur Milledieu to the others!'

'Lucky Monsieur Milledieu! Lucky others!' mumbled Georges, who was fiddling with an empty matchbox.

'*Try* to be nice for Mothers' Day!' pleaded Madame.

'You mean, I suppose, Day of Commerce, charged to the account of sentimentalists among the People!'

Madame took a handkerchief from her sleeve, and dabbed at her eyes.

'Taunts, nothing but taunts, Georges! I'm going back to the kitchen to help Lucienne!'

'And this is André,' continued her husband. 'André had his First Communion today, didn't you, André?'

André, dressed like a member of the Ku Klux Klan, would not look up from a comic he was reading.

'Stand up at once, André, and say hello to Monsieur Milledieu, a business contact of Lucienne's.'

André shrugged his shoulders.

'Where's your missal?' I inquired.

'Dunno!'

Monsieur Farouchette despaired. 'Lucienne! Lucienne!' he called into the kitchen. 'Come and say good morning to your gentleman friend!—Oh, I forgot Michèle, our younger daughter.'

She was wearing brown culottes, and found the nose she was picking more engrossing than myself.

Lucienne appeared. She kissed me.

'How wonderful to see you again, Toby! I was whisking Oeufs à la Neige for Mother. After all, this *is* her day!' She took her father's hand. 'Daddy has bought her the most fabulous present. A mixing machine! Wasn't he kind!'

Full marks! I do so admire those who make it a point of honour not to let the family down. Lucienne was acquiring style! She had restored my confidence.

At lunchtime, politics could not be kept at bay beyond the plat de résistance. Georges sarcastically informed us there was talk at the Fac that Professor Godon had actually spoken to a workman. He proposed the health of both of them, and then of the reformers.

'And now,' said his father uncomfortably, 'with the champagne he has so generously given, let us drink to Monsieur Milledieu!'

It was my turn. Could I do less than raise my glass to a Head of State?

'Le Général de Gaulle!'

The militant was beside himself.

'Long live Danny the Red and Chairman Mao!' he expostulated, picking up a sugar bowl of thickest china and flinging it at the opposite wall where it splintered a bottled galleon. 'Long live Jacques Sauvageot and Alain Geismar! To the devil with the pig de Gaulle!!'

'I'll have you know, young man, that "that pig" as you call him was forced to resign in 1946 because his programme was too revolutionary!'

'I don't give a f—— about 1946! Can't you and the General dig a hole and pull the earth in over yourselves and your f——ing memories?'

'I am not as old as you appear to believe.'

'You're too old to be pawing my sister—that's a fact!'

'Georges!!' Madame Farouchette dabbed her eyes again.

'Apologize to Monsieur Milledieu at once!' demanded the father. 'Lucienne's future is in his hands!'

' "In his hands" is just about it—the dirty old man!'

Lucienne abandoned her helping of Oeufs à la Neige and careered from the house.

'I'm sick of this dump, sick of it!' she yelled.

I followed her along the pathway in order to console her. I could hear her father shouting, 'What will Monsieur Milledieu think! Don't add more to this shit of a situation, you silly bitch! Come back this instant!' Her mother was wailing either 'Ma fête! Ma fête!' or 'Ma tête! Ma tête!'

Lucienne had rushed through the gate, and past some houses on an incline to a waste patch dotted with wild broom. I stumbled after.

'I hate them! I hate them!' she sobbed, pummelling the ground. 'Not just Georges, *all* of them! A well brought up man like you, Toby, must think us so ill-mannered!'

I was deeply touched. I lay down beside her.

'My darling! Calm yourself! I'll get you away from here as soon as possible.'

'But you haven't even got a motor car!'

'Yes I have!' The lie was deliberate. I hoped, thereby, to bring her back to reason.

'Take me away from here tonight! To Dôle, to Dijon, Paris, anywhere!!'

'You know that that's impossible! Your parents could have a warrant issued for our arrest! Abduction is a serious crime. Later—everything can happen later. Meanwhile it's essential your mother and father are on our side. At heart, they're decent, kindly people.'

'You don't love me!'

'You know that isn't true!'

'You don't love me! I've given you every chance to prove it!'

'There's more to love than that! I beseech you to control yourself, Lucienne!'

Monsieur and Madame Farouchette had by now caught up with us.

'She's hysterical—though little wonder!' I explained. I pretended to be hurt by her brother's behaviour, but I was exultant within. Lucienne had begged me to rescue her.

'You're acting like a slut! On the floor again . . . We thought that just this once . . .' Her father caught her by the arm. 'You're ruining your mother's day! You know she was depending on your support to see her through! Come back home this minute! What will the neighbours think if they see you in this state? It'll hardly bring me any extra business as their electrician!'

The four of us trailed down the hill and crept indoors.

I offered to help with the washing-up.

'The idea of an homme d'affaires washing up!' remonstrated Madame. 'Leave it to Lucienne!'

'Very well! But to turn to the other matter . . . I'd have thought Georges was the culprit. He didn't have to react to my toast the way he did.'

'I'm not defending my son's behaviour. Not for a moment,' replied Monsieur Farouchette. 'Will you join me on the terrace where we can talk in greater privacy?'

I complied, though I longed to join hands with Lucienne beneath the suds.

'Lucienne is a problem. She maximises the tantrums of others to draw attention to herself. She couldn't enter for the Bac—as much, I'm afraid, for lack of discipline as for lack of an academic bent. Now she's frustrated. She can obtain no Beaux Arts diploma, she feels she will never rise above her humble station. As it was, she only got her job as assistant at the Bon Marché because I once installed a fridge for the manager's wife.'

'I consider your fatherly interest in her welfare most commendable. But it was very wrong of you just now to deal with her so harshly!'

'Forgive me, Monsieur. I am not a saint. Nor am I disinterested. I have been too close too long. That is where you might help me. If I might make so bold . . .'

'Me?' I feigned surprise. I had already guessed his train of thought. Was I not contriving that he turn to me for counsel?

'Allow me to pour you an eau de vie.'

'So kind! Your good health, sir!'

'And yours! To return to what we were discussing . . . Do you think, as you have obviously discovered in Lucienne qualities I had not suspected, do you think you could see your way to finding her a job that will widen her horizons, give her more scope, enable her to travel? Forgive me asking, but is Monsieur married?'

'I am not, regrettably, in that happy state.'

'Might not then the interest you are taking in my daughter

be misconstrued? But it's presumptuous of me to assume you have any interest in her beyond the ordinary!'

'By no means, Monsieur Farouchette! Young people have always interested me greatly. Have no qualms on that score!'

'You mean you are agreed?'

'I'm a very busy man. I would have to know her better than I do. A fortnight's acquaintance is not enough. She would have to be groomed . . .'

'How long will you be in Besançon?'

'As long as I care to remain. I'm not anxious to return to Paris and its revolution!'

'Paris!! Dare I hope you might eventually find my daughter work there?'

'Nothing is impossible!'

'Monsieur . . . Monsieur . . .'

'The pleasure is mine. It isn't often one gets the opportunity to help a young girl in this way. But, as I said, it will take time. She will need guidance. I shall have to see much more of her during the coming days. Meanwhile, do you think that I might talk with her alone this afternoon?'

'But naturally! I had assumed you would be staying for the festivities this evening. Maybe the two of you would care to take a stroll?'

'An excellent idea! But give me your word you will never reveal to Lucienne the substance of our conversation!'

'Monsieur, I was going to ask the same of you! The slightest suspicion of collusion and the pauvre petite would take fright.'

Liberté! My mind was set ablaze with joyful preparations for the future.

Hand in hand, Lucienne and I walked down the narrow lane-ways that lead to Morre.

There is a heaven, I thought, from where Annie is ever watching over, fulfilling herself through her successor. I am alive again. Annie is alive in Lucienne . . .

We reached the rolling meadows beneath Notre Dame des Buis.

'Let's worship up there together!'

'You are a silly! Any worshipping will be done right here!' She dropped down among the wild forget-me-nots.

The Earth stood still, fearful for the honour of this supine child of nature. The birds, and crickets too, fell silent as if they dared not lullaby such innocence in jeopardy. 'Have no fears! I shall not harm her!' I promised, and, reassured, they continued with their minstrelsy.

'Was there much bombing here during the war?'

'How would I know?'

I knew the answer to my own question. The Virgin and Child above us commemorated the region's safety—save for the Allies' attack upon the Gare Viotte.

'You take no interest in your surroundings, the history of the province?'

'Get lost! Who wants to talk of history?'

'I do!'

'How boring!'

'Won't you accept me as I am?' I risked.

'I could ask the same myself. You never treat me like a man that loves me ought to.'

'You must be patient.'

'Patient for how long? You're not the only fish in the sea!'

'We must try to transcend the physical, darling!'

I kissed her knee.

'It's been like this for days now—Ludo, reading, kissing knees . . .'

'We must learn one another's interests . . .'

'Merde! Kiss me! Kiss me like a real man—like Tarzan!'

'Not here! Please not here! Someone may see us . . .'

'But there's not a soul . . .'

'Tourists stand with binoculars . . .'

'Poor Toby!'

'I wish you'd pronounce it right. The "o" is not open. It's closed like in "rôle".'

She tried. She worked hard.

'There!' I kissed her on the forehead. 'That's for being a good girl!'

'And if I go on working hard? If I go on working hard, you'll give me more than a kiss?'

'One day.'

Her face clouded.

I produced another present from my pocket.

'Perfume!' She accepted it delightedly.

The cloud passed.

'Hadn't we better be getting home? We've come a long, long way. Your parents will be worrying.'

'To hell with my parents! I've got you now to take care of me!'

Her words rang in my ears throughout the evening celebrations.

A paper cloth was laid. Neighbours arrived. Grown-ups helped young ones to stuff their napkins in their collars, and poured them a little wine and cut their coldmeats before the ratatouille and girdle-cake. In the absence of Georges, there was no talk of politics. There were toasts to mesdames, after which the table was set aside for party pieces—'Les Deux Gendarmes', the story of 'Goldilocks', a guitar solo and a religious poem. Gifts and posies were presented next, whereupon we ate biscuits and ice-cream and sang 'Michael Rowed the Boat Ashore' . . .

What a contrast this domestic scene to the political furore of the morrow!

A crowd of five thousand met in the Place St Pierre at 3.00 p.m. Teachers and students complimented their comrades-the-workers. Workers complimented their comrades-the-teachers and the students. Capitalism must be destroyed. The Teachers Federation proclaimed that the 'struggle' initiated by the Action Committee of the Fac must be protracted. Only a Communist trade union representative warned against provocateurs, by several hundred of whom I happened to be surrounded, all of them whistling and catcalling, and all of whom, at the end of the meeting, cut away from the rest and marched on the Préfecture carrying a red banner. There they painted swastikas on the gates, hurled iron bolts over the top and exploded a molotov cocktail, while Georges Farouchette and some other shaggy brethren applied themselves to smashing a wooden panel with a large plank discovered on a construction site nearby.

Notice of a nine o'clock meeting at the Fac was pushed into my hand as I returned disgustedly to my hotel.

To avoid the students, I dined not at the canteen but at the simple Foyer du Soldat on noodle soup, and steak and chips and salad. There was talk of the army waiting anxiously in reserve to back the police.

Later, curiosity got the better of me. I hastened to the meeting at the Fac for fear I had condemned the student body in its totality because of the work of its unrulier elements.

Standing by the temporary billboards or sitting on the bonnets of other people's motorcars, militants were wrangling in the court-yard. A white-helmeted service d'ordre passed among us wield-ing truncheons. At nine we moved in to the Cloché lecture-room. The wooden tiers around the table where the Comité d'Action was to deliberate were soon packed tight. Committee members bit on pipe-stems, sucked at Gaulloises, chewed gum; one worried a roll of bread to demonstrate he cared about essentials.

'No spectators!' someone urged as the throng increased. 'Com-mitted militants only!'

Those who were forced to stand for lack of space were chant-ing 'To Donzelot! To Donzelot'—an amphitheatre where all might sit in comfort.

Someone banged a bottle on the table and achieved temporary silence. Tobacco smoke hovered between tense, tanned faces, red pullovers, shirtsleeves, spectacles, mackintoshes, and then soared up towards the lampshades.

'To Donzelot! To Donzelot!' The demand was resumed.

'Fascists! Fascists!' returned those already seated.

The bottle was banged again. A committee member in a tennis jersey conferred with colleagues. A transfer was agreed upon. We filed to our new quarters where the Chairman promptly raised the first item on the agenda.

To my relief, the attack on the Préfecture was denounced from the platform.

Georges Farouchette was scandalized.

A skinny female scar-face shrieked, 'Ta gueule, lapin!'

Uproar.

'Tais-toi!' from the speaker.

'Sous-merde!' from the arena.

Raucous laughter before resumption of discourse.

Speech after speech. Irrelevant. Irrelevant to orphans of war. Irrelevant to prison welfare, to my squalid hotel room, to paying my debts. Irrelevant to loving.

A dark and sallow curly-head, in baggy trousers and a black needle-cord jacket, had now taken the platform and was arrang-ing his notes. His name was Bernard Lhomme. The boy in the

84

tennis jersey moved to make room for him. He was warmly applauded for his sentiments. He demanded wider perspectives for women in society. Why, he asked, should women workers be paid less than men?

All clapped loudly as he stood down.

More speeches.

Bernard Lhomme returned. He bent down to whisper something to his comrade in the tennis jersey. Was there something he forgot to say? The audience gasped. He was lunging to the platform floor. He was dragged from the hall.

Clichés concerning class and democracy continued, punctuated by savage vulgarities and the Chairman's fist banging on the table. The audience grew restless. Girls and cigarettes were shared as abstractions were propounded and compounded—manifestation, orientation, organization, occupation, réoccupation, protestation, informations, solutions, localization, mobilization, contestation, rénovation, explication, concentration, proposition, innovation, situation, formation, répression, révolution, contrerévolution, progression, provocation, prédiction, revendications, insurrection, mutation, moralization . . .

A longhaired Cassius is now condemning, at length and in turn, each proposal made by a committee of Communist professors for the reform of the university.

He is signalled to stop.

'Bernard is dead,' the youth in the tennis jersey announces quietly.

Spontaneously the assembly rises and stands in silence.

The youth in the tennis jersey leaves the platform, weeping openly.

The hall empties. Still not a word is spoken.

Huddled groups whisper in the courtyard.

'Bernard is dead.'

'It seems impossible, Bernard is dead.'

'His mother! Where does his mother live?'

'Someone must go to her!'

Theories are forgotten. Something personal has happened, something real. Something has touched the students' hearts. A friend is dead. They have lost a friend.

Until this moment I despised them. Henceforward I am prepared to offer some respect.

I slip back into the empty theatre. I climb to the platform and, between the photographs of Marx and Lenin, address a thousand unseen faces:

'Since my arrival at Besançon, six weeks ago, I have watched your behaviour with disgust—in the TV room and restaurant of the Cité as well as on the streets. I am aware that Liberty plants both elbows on the table, but this is too much! You claim that, against your will, you have been made into an élite, set apart from your brothers, the workers. Let me tell you, *they* are the élite! Show me the factory canteen where strangers are pushed for delaying at the counter! Show me the one where elderly ladies, exhausted and confused after travelling many hundreds of miles, are humiliated and reviled! Tell me! Do workers blow pipe-smoke in the faces of their comrades while they eat? Do they belch, throw crusts, spit water, bang their jugs, make love, leave half their food uneaten? Do they scatter leaflets on the ground for others to sweep tidy? Do they steal ahead of their brothers in the queue? Well *do* they? I'm waiting! But you remain silent. And why do you remain silent? You remain silent because you are ashamed. You remain silent because you know what I say is true. In England we speak of the Dignity of Labour. What is so shocking in France at the present time is that you, in the name of democracy, are robbing Labour of all its dignity. Do you not perceive that sexual immaturity has unbalanced you? Do you *seriously* advocate that those who are your match in brain power should share your privileges? If so, who would build and service the institutions of Utopia? Boo to your hearts' content! I have by no means finished yet. Booing with you has become a habit. You boo your President, do you not? The question was rhetorical. You mime his gestures. You make light of his sentiments. What more can a man do? In all humility he has placed his destiny in public hands: by way of referendum he will obtain a mandate for renewal of his leadership or for its termination. Do you really believe your views will count when expressed in a torrent of orgasmic rage? Can't you indulge your sensuality in private? Do mass demonstrations, does marching through the streets with banners bearing specious slogans, appeal to the best or to the worst components of society? It breaks my heart to see, as I have done, a pretty cowgirl traduced through your example into tramping the streets demanding justice for the farmers. Oh yes, you laugh! To mention anything so natural as a pretty cowgirl is a cue for merriment. I have my little weakness. But that is funny. That is unimportant. What doesn't concern *you* can be treated lightly. Because you've got your sleeping partners on the campus, the likes of me can be ignored. Carry on! Split your sides with laughter! One future day, though, you will recall that you were in training at the taxpayer's expense, and that the objects of your education were simplicity, seriousness, modesty, industry and a devotion to public service. When you've finished hooting, I will continue. I myself . . . There is still someone hooting . . . I myself cannot claim to be faultless. I am open to temptation. But, as an older man, I intend to give you some advice. That is my duty. It is for you to choose then how to act. You have free will.

I admit that, till this evening, I've been prejudiced against you. But your humane reaction to the death of Bernard Lhomme has convinced me that a rapprochement is now possible. Now that you, too, have experienced personal tragedy, we can start to build on common ground. I, too, you see, have suffered. I lost, when I was young, younger even than you, someone who was very, very dear to me. Thank you for your attention! Yes, I can see that you are not really bad. I had thought I could never share with you my heart and soul. I thought you were too cynical, too sophisticated, too mocking. I was wrong. I have seen tonight one of your leaders shedding tears. I withdraw my condemnation.

No, don't get up to go! I will be brief.

Picture an only child seeking solace from a serving wench. I dare a kiss and, having dared a kiss, I ask for more. I lose her in war, a moment prior to fulfilment. Then, now, incredibly, here, in Besançon, I find her, young as ever. No need to whistle. Let us call a truce. Let me freely revel in my honeymoon. Reopen your public buildings! Allow me unashamedly to show Lucienne your tapestries and treasured volumes! No, hear me out! Return to your studies. Encourage the dustmen to empty the bins. Enable me to ramble and make love beneath the breastwork of the Citadelle without the stench of garbage floating to my nostrils!

One other matter. Disease runs rife throughout the land. Desist from indiscriminate copulation. Set my dear one an example.
In return I offer you the hand of friendship.
Thank you.
Goodnight.'

6

Monday, 10th June

Quicksands. Whom to admire? Whom to trust? Can I even trust myself? If not, have I the right to expect my enemies to be consistent?

I had proffered the hand of friendship to the students. It was the workers who agreed to take it : they emptied the dustbins.

I, on my side, continued to show goodwill. I spoke at dinner to a redhead agitator.

'Whose camp are you in now?'

'I'm deaf to your absurdities, old fool!'

On the 30th May, after the decision of their President not to abdicate, a band of bourgeois hearties drove a cavalcade of car-tanks through the centre of the town and, sporting tricolor ribbons and sounding their klaxons to the rhythm of 'L'Algérie Française', mounted a pavement and gave the V-sign to a workman before wounding him with a shotgun in the arm. At which, the militants panicked and, after parading there with crowbars, blocked the entrance to the Fac and waited till the chimes of midnight before defenestrating their internees onto a roadway iced with broken glass.

The 31st boded no better.

Students obstructed the path of Gaulliste marchers. Insults and counter-insults were exchanged in the rue de la République.

'De Gaulle au poteau!'

'Communistes à Moscou! Le jour de gloire est arrivé . . . marchons . . . marchons . . .'

The church of St Pierre and the Hôtel de Ville were desecrated with the words 'REVOLUTION, NON AUX NEGOTIA-TIONS' and the dreaded initials 'CRS-SS'.

89

Pigeons wheeled as fire-engines drove at speed to scatter vociferous crowds. The students, believing, no, hoping they had been attacked, raced, brandishing batons, to the rue Mégevand where they built a barricade to the derision of chefs and sous-chefs from the Palais de la Bière. Traffic was inconvenienced. The Mayor, with courtesy, requested a dispersal, to no avail. The police threw grenades. The so-called revolutionaries withdrew, thereby vouching for their insincerity. Their bluff was called.

Meanwhile, I attempted to gratify Lucienne. I allowed her to render me rubescent with unwonted friction with the compliance of a priest who has only partly found his faith and must nonetheless distribute wine and wafers during Holy Communion.

I would ask some cultural question to divert her mind.

'Which of the Catholic novelists do you prefer?'

She was quietened for an instant, but would then again resort to her one obsession.

'Love me!'

I persisted :

'Cayrol? Quéffelec?'

'Love me!'

'Anne Huré?'

She ran her fingertips around her breasts and down her thighs.

'Take me! Take me!'

I took her—to the pictures.

How to raise this nubile shopgirl from the herd—above the pimply students selling 'Le Pavé', above the Kelton factory workers still rampaging through the streets, above the Algerian strikers queueing for the dole? It was my duty to curb her profligate desires, subject them to valuable disciplines, or she, too, might run amok. I was certain she was not beyond redemption. She was my task in life, the purpose of my journeyings. In her I hoped to find eventual release. But I rebuffed her whinnying appeals. Again and again I repulsed her attempts to make me mount her. Bridling her frisky protests, stroking her tossing mane, thwarting each rebellious manoeuvre, I reined her aside.

Was I deceiving her? Due to years of living, albeit defiantly, in the shadow of intimidation, was I incapable of providing a less arid régime than dalliance and idle boasting? Like the students, was I ill-equipped to carry to a logical conclusion the events I had deliberately induced? As they were playing soldiers, was Toby Mildew playing soupirant?

I nerved myself to be constructive. 'Not before we are man and wife!' I replied, when next she begged for satisfaction.

She threw her arms passionately about me.

'Elope with me to Paris!'

'There, there! Calm yourself! We must think clear-headedly! I do not, dear child, propose to indulge in a hurried, madcap escapade!'

I was penniless. I needed time for reflection, though of one thing I was certain: I would rather kill myself than do Lucienne the wrong that Wordsworth did Annette Vallon.

The revolution fell away.

Workers declared the students' idea to have been their bread. The Ladies could buy again their weeklies at the Maison de la Presse. Schools were filled with the ring of children's voices. Policemen strutted, peacock confident. Recipients of mail excitedly shook hands with postmen, then hurried to drop answers into letter-boxes, too long starved. Cleaners briskly removed last vestiges of propaganda. Soldiers quaffed beer and toyed once more with girlfriends around the Ecole de Ponts; and, though the area was lorry-lined and still marked off as a Zone Militaire, the woolly dogs, the harriers, the boy who cleaned his bicycle and the wife who rocked her pram returned to join obstinate anglers who had ignored the rumpus.

Though there was football on the lawn of the Faculté des Lettres, and someone lounged there on a lilo, the conduct of the students showed signs of amelioration. A television interview with General de Gaulle, received at first with the usual mimicry and laughter, was eventually accorded a respectful hearing. Ionesco's dictum was proved true—a revolution is a turning back, a re-appraisal.

To celebrate the 'return to sanity', as Fay described it, I was invited by the Ladies to a party at the lodgings of Miss Patsy Jones.

On arrival, I presented Olive Brownlow with a bouquet of roses picked at risk from the Micaud Promenade. I was offered a sherry in return.

'I am sure, Ladies, that you have progressed sufficiently to speak to me tonight only in French!' I remarked disingenuously.

'It would be ill-advised of us to compete with someone who has made France and things French the study of a lifetime!' countered Miss Farley of Bath.

'Jolly well put!' agreed Miss Moxey, in over-played relief.

Looking from one guest to the other, I wondered whom to approach discreetly for another loan.

'A Fondue Franc-Comtoise!'

Fay placed it on a matted side-table to applause and cheering.

Olive Brownlow, busy with the wine, diminished her friend's moment of glory with ill-timed criticism:

'Don't be silly, Fay! You *know* that's wrong. One puts it in the centre of the floor—we all sit round it on our cushions! Mr M., come help uncork these bottles, while the rest go collect their forks and plates and serviettes!'

We were all soon dipping cubes of bread into bubbling Gruyère. My palate was disappointed. Fay had added too much garlic, and I could taste Kirsch at the expense of vin d'Alsace.

After entremets and coffee, I offered to assist with the kitchen chores.

'As the only male guest! Certainly not!' remonstrated Miss Brownlow, plumping me a pouffe to rest my back on. 'Make yourself comfortable! In a moment some of us are going to perform charades, aren't we, girls?' She made signs to them to prepare, and Wendolyn Moxey, in her element, ran to collect props and mark out positions.

'Can't *I* join in the fun?'

'After all our rehearsals on your behalf! Please don't disappoint us, Mr M.!'

She explained that three tableaux were to be performed, adding up, in a fourth, to a phrase which I must try to guess.

'An entertainment all for me?'

'All for you, Mr Mildew!'

'Ladies, I am flattered!'

Miss Jones, for Scene One, ambled back and forth and around what must be a Baghdad bazaar. She handled articles at different stalls, only to reject them one by one. What was she after? Something of one syllable. A quilt? A shawl? No, something smaller. A brooch? A pendant? . . . Suddenly something caught her fancy. A vendor climbed onto a stool and lifted it off a hook. Miss Jones ran it through her fingers, carried it to the light, examined it on either side. It apparently sufficed—but only just, for she shrugged her shoulders and paid with a great show of reluctance before marching off the stage.

Scene Two equally confounded me. Miss Westbright was in charge of a line of Gaiety Girls—or perhaps they were dolls from 'La Boutique Fantasque'. She led them in turn to the centre of the room and arranged them on the carpet in the form first of the letters NO and then US. United States? 'No' to the United States? I was lost. Was this due to lack of practice? I hadn't played charades since I was at the orphanage.

'I give up!' I cried.

'Wait for Scene Three!' They silenced me, whereupon each of the actresses looked happily about her and, laden with bags and boxes, rushed straight into the welcoming arms of Miss Alicia Farley (Headmistress? Mother?) who poured them something from what might be a gigantic samovar.

' "Scarf-dolls-pot"? "Shop-no-tea"? I haven't an idea!'

'The finale, then!' commanded Miss Brownlow, adding in my ear, 'The three words put together form our message.'

The complete cast assembled before me, with Miss Jones, Miss Westbright and Miss Farley in the foreground.

At a nod from Miss Brownlow, all, with the expressions and vivacity of termagants, waved clenched fists in my direction.

Miss Brownlow halted them, then turned to me with an expectant 'We-ell?!!'

They waited breathless.

I remained mute.

Finally, Fay burst out, 'Oh, is this really fair to Mr Mildew, Olive?!'

'Fair to *Mr Mildew*!!' intoned Miss Jones, Miss Westbright and Miss Farley in unison.

And the outraged trio waved their clenched fists at me again, beating the air in rhythm to the words 'Pay Us Back!!', which they now, deserting mime, bawled aloud till Miss Brownlow barked, 'The message must be plain!' and, while the rest looked on, demanded restitution.

I did not play Hamlet's uncle. I did not call for lights. I answered them calmly:

'Restitution? I do not understand, Miss Brownlow! Restitution of what?'

Bedlam.

'A common criminal!'

'We should have recognized you from the outset!'

'We had our suspicions!'

'We saw you examining underwear!'

'Nasty!'

'Depraved!'

'We gave you your chance!'

'We adopted you!'

'And then you duped us!'

'You abused our charity!'

'I always said you were unsavoury!'

'I saw you lusting at the piscine!'

'I saw you touch a girl at Amancey!'

'I saw you on the dodgems!'

'Yes, and with a mere child!'

'Loathsome!'

'Vile!'

'Degenerate!'

'And I went so far as to lend you fifty francs!'

'So did I!'

'I lent *sixty*!'

'Bloodsucker!'

'Of how many others do you take advantage?'

'What are the depths to which you will not sink!'

'You are a disgrace to your sex!'

Insinuations and accusations stabbed me from every side.

I requested silence. I told them I deplored their hasty judgment. I excused one among them only—Fay who, since our meeting by the riverside, had remained a loyal friend and tonight had not raised her voice against me. Now she was weeping, beseeching her unnatural partner to show me clemency.

'Yes, I have been to prison . . .' I explained.

'There! What did I tell you!'

'I knew as much!'

'. . . With that I cannot argue. I pleaded guilty—but only on advice . . .'

'Where there's smoke there's fire!'

94

'The man's a maniac!'

'He should be flogged!'

'You mean castrated!'

'May I be permitted to speak to those who have charged me with financial dishonesty?'

'Go ahead then, but make it short!'

'I shall ask two questions. Were not your loans in return for services rendered? Have I ever suggested that you would not be repaid in full?'

'The banks opened three days ago!'

'Yes, three *days*, ladies! Have you not heard of the three days grace? If I'd had any idea you were in such urgent need . . .'

'Very well, Mr Mildew! Three days grace! But, here in France, I am responsible for the welfare of your creditors. I insist that you repay them by Monday and no later!'

'There is no need to insist, Miss Brownlow! I am a gentleman, and a gentleman is as good as his word. Had I known the ladies concerned were in such a sorry plight, I would have paid them back as soon as feasible, I do assure you. They shall have their money, that I guarantee, within three days.'

I got up to go.

'Not so fast, Mr Mildew! I shall require a written undertaking.'

'I am afraid, Miss Brownlow, I do not give undertakings other than verbal. They have always been good enough for others, so why not you as well?'

'In that case we shall call the police. Patsy, go to the phone at once!'

'No, Olive!' shouted Fay. 'How can you be so cruel!'

'Very well! If by Monday evening this blackguard has not sent what he owes us to this address, he shall reap the bitter consequences!'

'And mind how you treat that girl!' added Mrs Slatter.

'That girl, I'll have you know, is my future wife!!'

'Which girl?'

Miss Westbright's barb and a contrapuntal 'Yes, which girl!!', 'Which!!', 'Go on! Tell us which!!' hammered in my ears as I took my leave.

It was already Friday. I must not pawn the simple ring I had bought for Lucienne so we could plight our troth on Sunday in the Queen's Tower of the Citadelle. Nor could I approach her father for remittances if I was not to lose her.

Praying for guidance, my mind in turmoil, I tramped through the Old Town. I squatted to defecate in the nearest alleyway. To left and right, the twisted roofs of blue-tinged hovels invested my mood of apprehension with a runic prescience which augured catastrophe.

The moon circled high above me.

A roulette wheel!

I saw it now! Maman, the reckless bird of night who haunted the Côte d' Azur each season with an extravagance that left me destitute upon her death, was not a barren memory to be banished from the bounds of consciousness. No! Rather was her vice a guide-light signalling my rescue. Tomorrow, in the Casino de Besançon, with my last francs, I would unleash my inherited instincts, not to my own detriment, not as the drunkard takes his liquor, but to the advantage of the ones that harassed me.

Lack-lustre couples were still dining on the terrace of the Casino when I reached there. I cursed my lot—the subterfuges and the pretences which their kind imposed upon me since I lost my childhood Amorette. Their obduracy, their unchallenged arrogance, their parsimony, their crude generalizations, made it my duty to outwit them. Intimidation breeds recalcitrance.

I experienced an admixture of fear and guilt. The relics of my father's woodwork were symbols of application to a valuable craft. By coming here tonight, I was travelling back in time in order to summon the improvidence of my mother and insult the example of his solemn industry.

To assuage my anguish and to fuse my fragmented emotions into a profitable whole, I ordered a treble brandy. The bar was in semi-darkness. Couples coagulated, inched round the dance-floor, toffee-slow. These besmirched and willing lackeys of carnality would be the first to cast stones at Toby Mildew, though his devotion to Lucienne was unsullied and he had never asked for more of her than a grateful protégée's wistful kiss of reverence.

The barmaid was presumptuous:

'Monsieur is lonely?'

'I take water in my brandy, never soda!'

'Monsieur is angry. This is not the place to come if Monsieur is angry. My bar is a happy place for happy people.'

I surveyed in the obscurity the cheek by jowl ellipses that balanced on a shoulder of each partner. I scrutinized their lugubrious expressions for a single instant's vitality, for a flicker of what lies beyond the wallowing hog's ideas of love.

'These people are happy?'

'Happy in forgetfulness.'

She smiled and pressed a switch. Ultra-violet light flooded the room. Synthetic fabrics at once became diaphanous, lingerie overt. Roués pinched and pointed. Coquettes made hasty pretence of modesty. The commotion suggested a What the Butler Saw during the rutting season in a deer-park.

With a flick of the wrist, the barmaid returned her domain to its status quo. The excitement dwindled.

'You have power over others, Madame!'

'Not over you, Monsieur!' she answered shrewdly.

I forgave her forwardness. She was stating a fact, not for the sake of insolence, not with the frivolous guesswork of the average hussy, but as a scientist who nightly views his specimens with meticulous resignation. If she had been twenty years younger, I would have asked her her name.

'Here on business?'

'No.'

I let it go at that. She didn't deserve to be burdened with the sadness of my story.

I offered my passport to the clerk outside the gaming room. 'Name?... Date of birth?... Place of birth?... Profession?... Permanent address?... Present address?...' I was a youth in the vestibule of his first brothel. No madam ever served so timorous a customer as did that clerk. Behind him lay hidden the moss-clad tables, the wheels which tonight would be my salvation or my crucifixion. Lady Luck, no doubt, prepared herself within, crimping her tousled locks and spraying her raddled breasts in readiness for the novice she must educate.

The inner sanctum was revealed to me. The door re-closed.

My stomach liquefied. So much depended on this indiscretion. Winner would take all—impress his sweetheart, pay his hotel bill, recover his honour. Loser would be flung into a maelstrom of calamities from which he might never re-emerge.

D 97

My worldly goods, including borrowings, were two hundred and thirty francs. I boldly changed them into chips, and took a copy from a pile of printed rules to pilot me.

Roulette! How often had I heard my mother speak the word! How seldom had I paid attention! If only I had demanded explanations, shared her euphoria and despair! If only I had begged to accompany her where palm trees fan the most infamous casinos in the world! The types of bet, their odds, were easy enough to master. Of necessity, the intricacies eluded me. Was it wise to punt on colour as well as number? What were the systems? Words from my mother's vocabulary—'partager', 'Martingale', 'Labouchère'—scolded me sternly for having snubbed them. I was shipwrecked and I had never learned to swim.

Best learn the outcome fast! I sat myself down and placed my chips—four 50's, three 10's—in two small heaps before me. The chef-de-partie dismissed my significance with a cursory glance. A simpleton at large among the skilful, I blushed at my disgrace. The croupier raked in, threw, thrust forward a host of discs of differing colours, and, but for the hands that shot out swiftly to place them on the figured columns, their sober, concentrating owners might have been waxwork dummies or carcasses embellished by some overnice mortician.

'Rien ne va plus!'—I had not betted, and the turn was nearly over.

Rattle of ivory on brass. Metallic oscillation. Silence. 'Deux, noir, pair et manque!' Raking in. Paying out. The atmosphere corrupts me. I become electrified and vigilant. With beginner's recklessness I play 50 en carré—and lose it! With beginner's disappointment I long to run into my mother's skirts or lay my head on Lucienne's bosom.

Through a veil of tears, I place two 10's and 50 en colonne. The 50 has it! I am richer than when I started. Maman! Lucienne! Be the first to share the news! I shall buy you each a pretty present! I owe it to you. You have both been good to me. You above all, maman, must be rewarded for giving me this talent! Through you, my instinct grasps the processes of number without the need of conscious calculation. In this, the region where I once ignored you, I now bless your name!

There!—100 on three numbers en transversale—16, 17, 18.

Why this delay?! Tourneur, set the wheel spinning! Send that little ball to do its duty! Who cares about the bets of other players, automata who can no longer recall the beauty of the passion which has led to their debasement! The difference between their first experience and mine is that tonight for Toby is an extremity which, whatever its irksome cause, will kindle a process of healing and not a pitiful dégringolade.

'Vingt-deux, noir, pair et passe!'

What of it! One win, one lose! Nature must often refresh herself, gird up her loins before new acts of bounty! The breeze must blow, the leaves must shudder before the rising of the mellowing sun!

50 en carré on 22's neighbours. 'Rein ne va plus!' Run your race, little bead! The dawn chorus: Daphnis and Chloë: the conductor's baton slices downwards: 21. A win! A win! The rake pushes the neat pile towards me. This is sublime!!

Again the wheel is turning. My mother's blood is tingling in my veins, alcoholized by the fire that annually consumed her, that fire which, after years of resistance, now holds me in its thrall. Provençal fire of poppy red and scorching black! Her face at the pivot, at the Holy Cross, shines forth from the burnished brass! She beckons me. La Belle Dame Sans Merci. Take, eat, this is my body. You are my body. Suffer the little children. I am your child, your obedient child. You hypnotize and I obey. Oui, maman! Tout ce qui te plaira! One hundred francs? No? Three hundred? Five hundred and ten? My all, Not ten? The ten is vulgar? Five hundred francs?

She nods.

And now she is in labour—squeezing, twisting, writhing, epileptic. The wheel is the medium coupling me to the agony of the message she would impart. The croupier soon will call a halt. We must hasten. Reach me, maman! Reach me! Reach out! Succour me in this hour of reckoning!

The clash of cymbals. The rending of the skies in twain. The number 28, the year of my birth, forces its head from the table. 'En plein! En plein!' my mother shrieks, and, as the croupier's lips part to uvulate the first consonant of his cessatory announcement, as his mouth stretches wide, I propel my wager to the date I was delivered into this life's purgatory.

A mistake!

I kick my chair back in alarm. With fingertips upon the felt, I lean incredulously towards the cauldron where maman has vanished.

A mistake! Rejected! Not what she wanted! The number 28 a puny hieroglyphic in the rigmarole of time!

Despised! Destroyed!

'Traitress! Murderess!' I wail.

Two doughfaced neighbours stare at me in consternation. They grab me by the shoulders. A burly official hastens over. I am led towards the door. My last ten francs is changed for me and pressed into my hand. I strain back towards the wheel, repeating, 'Traitress! Murderess!' I am dragged roughly along empty passages. I am cast out.

I was wakened on Sunday (yesterday), by the midday carillon of St Pierre.

I sipped the cold coffee, nibbled the stale bread on the tray which had been left beside me.

I would have drawn the curtains to lighten the monetary cares tormenting me had I not detected, among the peal of bells, the sound of voices. I lifted an edge. The patron and his daughter were standing in the courtyard. He picked her a marigold from the flower-patch beside his garage. Then he kissed her cheek and held her hand. It embittered me that he could so flaunt his natural feelings without recriminations.

I meditated on Lucienne. Would she leave me now that I was penniless, now that I could not afford to buy her gifts and take her to the haunts she favoured? Would an imitation diamond ring subdue her sexual demands till we were wed?

I waited until the incestuous couple had retired indoors and until the inevitable lunchtime hubbub round the kitchen table had begun before leaving my room and crossing the cobblestones out of hailing distance of further requests for rent.

Nimble in anticipation, I climbed the lanes of the Ville Haute. Above me, unclouded in the blue and green of the June afternoon, stood the sturdy acropolis, the lay Citadelle of the Roi Soleil, symbolizing the immensity, the permanence of my affection for Lucienne.

I reached my destination. Here, in the fifth century, with faith no greater than my own, pilgrims at Easter and at Whitsuntide foregathered to touch the shroud of St Etienne in the cathedral now replaced by Vauban's frontal pavilion where, along with Sunday's pleasure-seekers, I bought a ticket to go in. The umbrellas peeping over bastions, the childrens' games of the inner esplanade, the menagerie, the displays of ironwork, shells and marionettes, supported my analogy with rituals of the past, provided that aura of kermesse which accompanies so many religious undertakings. I myself was about to worship at the feet of one of God's children. I would admit to her my frailties, my predicament. My honesty would form a bedrock for our marriage. I could serve her, then, without misgivings until my death.

I mounted the steps to the Queen's Tower to savour the spot where my darling would be awaiting me in less than half an hour. Beyond the fenestrations lay a map of memories—the policeman's garden, the Ecole de Ponts, the road to Beure and Lyon . . . Warlike gnats, the jazzing of transistors, could not distract me. I thrilled at the prospect of confessing to the nymph-child of my dreams my tribulations.

To while away the last long minutes to our meeting, I walked to the menagerie with the palpitations of my over-eager heart resounding in my temples. How could the moufflons, marabous and bears show such disinterest! Or did I see a llama smile at my expectancy? Deep in their arid pit the black bears begged for morsels. Not for me such self-abasement! Lucienne would hear my troubles, then, like the pheasants here, murmur spontaneous comfort. No need for supplication when the breast-milk of her kindliness would yield me all the food I craved for.

I watched two monkeys picking one another's backs. Some leaped on a red and yellow wheel. Dizzily I looked aside. Against a backcloth of flamingoes, a soldier and his girl were patently degrading love's perfection. I could not focus in the sunlight. Perhaps I was wrong. Perhaps they were not guilty of indecency. I did not wish to do them an injustice. I shielded my eyes. My pupils accommodated. The picture clarified. Despite the jerky motion of the scarlet, longlegged creatures impairing the image, I affirmed I had not been mistaken. The girl turned away from her seducer. I stood transfixed. It was Lucienne! The soldier pleaded. She gestured towards the entrance. She was saying she must go. The soldier pointed to his watch. Wasn't there still time? She nodded . . .

I checked my base conjectures. My over-hasty conclusions reflected a tyrannical possessiveness which must at all costs be restrained. This moment in my life would be the ultimate test— of me as well as of her. I had not satisfied her physical desires. It was wrong to blame her if she petted. If I could overcome my impulse to drag her to a parapet and fling her to oblivion; if she could resist the temptation to desert the side of a rough fighter for the sake of someone who applauded peace and scholarship, our union would be the healthier. Both our metals would be refined by curbing ruder inclinations.

I watched Lucienne closely, denouncing the invisible waves of light and sound which could not accurately assist me, yet extolling them also for not informing her of my whereabouts and the lust for reprisal which must be raging on my countenance.

A common soldier in a beret engaging the attention of my loved one! I laughed the thought away, then sobered. A midinette might not have scruples. What if these perfunctory cuddles signified a previous connexion? Were they lovers? I caught my breath. Was this more than an idle hypothesis prompted by jealousy? Look! Were they not at ease together and blatantly compatible? The thighs that taxed his trousers, her busty blouse; his loose composure, her flighty tension—the two of them were sexual complements! I gaped in horror. I had been deceived. Her pulse when in my presence had been quickened at thought of lolling in some dullard's rough-hewn arms. The innocence of my intentions had blinded me to the wickedness of hers.

Again I turned to a kindlier interpretation. Was she not accepting these advances in pretence, to quench his ardour and to the easier escape him when the time arrived for our appointment? I watched to learn.

Lucienne still made excuses. The soldier still was pleading. He reached for his wallet. He handed her a note. She swept his hand away derisively and made as if to leave. Good girl! I do adore you! He offered her the same note doubled. Not interested? My angel!

Now he waved three. He leered abusively. He was certain, this time, of his money's sorcery.

I clung to the cage in consternation.

She snatched her price from him, and, as she did so, I moaned aloud.

'Did one of them bite you?' a woman inquired anxiously. 'You shouldn't hold the monkeys' cage!'

Lucienne was walking with her soldier to a piece of scrubland on the southern limits.

'Take your hand from there!' the woman was advising.

A crowd was gathering round me.

'He won't move! I've told him to take his hand away and he won't move! . . . Monsieur!!' She was shouting at me now. 'Monsieur!! The monkeys are dangerous! You'll be bitten again!!'

I wept.

'Come here!' She lifted down my hand and, with a tissue, tried to wipe away my tears. 'What can be the matter? Can't someone make him talk?'

A common whore! Lucienne sank down in distant grasses and, while a peacock split the heavens with its screeching, the soldier lowered himself on top of her.

The patron tapped at my door shortly after I had clambered between the sheets to ease my suffering. Obtaining no response, he used his duplicate key.

'The breakfast things?' I stretched to pass the tray.

'Enjoyed your afternoon?'

'Indeed yes! Disappointing, though, that the Musée des Beaux-Arts is still closed for repairs!'

'No doubt Monsieur has other interests apart from cultural ones.'

'I don't quite follow . . . If you have finished, I was resting and . . .'

'Would Monsieur first consider settling his account?'

'Sunday is hardly the occasion!'

'I agree. Yesterday was the occasion, but Monsieur seemed to forget it. So was the previous Saturday and the Saturday before that . . .'

'Mon patron, I am an English gentleman. If I say I will pay you, pay you I will!'

'I am not a moneylender. There are overheads . . .'

'If I'd known your position was insecure I would not have come here. The hotel is recommended.'

'So what does Monsieur propose?'

'I shall move to a hotel whose management will take me at my word.'

'Not before paying your arrears.'

'Of course not! I shall call on the bank in the morning. Until five days ago it was closed to all comers. You seem to forget that there has been a revolution!'

'Monsieur had better keep his promise. Otherwise I shall be forced to call the police.'

'Is it your habit to threaten guests in this crude manner?'

'I have been lenient, Monsieur. Monsieur has entertained a girl in his room. He once frightened my daughter. It will not be another hotel for you, Monsieur. It will be the rue Pergaud!'

'The rue Pergaud?'

'The location of our prison.'

I was again the wounded campaigner struggling to raise himself from off the battlefield.

'You would prevent me touch the hem of Amaryllis' skirt?'

'You have till tomorrow morning, Monsieur. Monsieur has been warned!'

These papers were confiscated by the police at the time of Mr Mildew's arrest.

NIGEL SOMEONE

For George Browne

'Wouldn't be a teacher . . . !'

Mr Bluett, replenishing his flask with Hennessy, gulped some, then lurched from the off-licence. He did not acknowledge the condescension of the manager. He was preoccupied. Unlike the other members of the staff of Adelaide Bing, he had received no Christmas card from Nigel. The slight, maliciously intended, dismayed him.

He enunciated 'Earl's Court!' as clearly as he could to forestall a discourteous 'What?!' from the ticket clerk inside the station.

'Bloody passengers! Haven't you nothing smaller than five quid?!'

'I'm sorry.'

A deluge of silver, and 'Hurry along! Next!' rewarded this politeness.

There were all too few, both in and out of school, to set the likes of Nigel an example. Even Lady Sandra when she took the boy for Nature—why did she merely smile every time he swore at her?

Insufficient emphasis on character formation—it wasn't hard to disinter the root cause of the State System's decline. It hardly seemed to matter to Muriel as headmistress, let alone to her underlings, that the Upper School parodied 'We three kings' again this year. "Star of wonder, Star of light, Charlie caught his pants alight . . ." Lizzie Oates and Colin Coote, the Deputy, hadn't attempted to stifle their own snickering. Wasn't it someone's duty to stem the rising tide of insubordination?

How far off the Forties when he and Muriel Hodge paraded the yard—or 'playground' as she now preferred to call it—planning a fairer world; when the spirit of Coalition lingered, and there was mutual respect between officers unashamed to wear a bowler and men unashamed to wear a bib and brace; when he, a gentleman lodging in Chelsea, could associate on almost equal terms with Muriel, a common Hackney girl; and when pupils heeded each of them admiringly!

Had it, after that Indian Summer of wishful thinking and the disastrous era of Public Welfare succeeding it, had it been frivolous to claim that any hope of future civility under the Pax Britannica now rested in a Nigel, and that Nigel must assume the White Man's Burden and start afresh to sow green fields of England everywhere?

From when Lady Sandra shepherded her class into Assembly on the first morning of the boy's first term, Mr Bluett had counted on the co-operation of this exquisite piccaninny.

'Who's that blubbing over there?' he inquired under cover of the latest folk-song, chosen for the gramophone by Colin Coote.

'Nigel someone . . . Already insisting on Free Dinners! I've explained that until I've evidence brought to me from Miss Hodge or the Secretary he'll have to pay or go without!'

'Send him to me afterwards, would you?'

Lady Sandra complied gratefully.

'What's all this about refusing to pay for dinner, Nigel?'

'Haven't any money.'

'I haven't any money, *sir.*'

'I haven't any money, *sir.*'

'That's better!' He took some loose change from his pocket. 'Take this, will you, to Miss Walsh, the School Secretary, till we find out what's to be done in future!'

Nigel hesitated.

'Quick, or you'll be late!'

Mr Bluett spoke with Miss Hodge at break—or 'playtime' as she called it now.

'Muriel, there seems to be some doubt over one of Lady Sandra's new-boys. Nigel someone. Is he entitled to Free Dinners or is he not?'

'Nigel? Most certainly! A desertion case and an only child. Mum has had to take a job in Tesco's.'

'Have you informed the Secretary or his class teacher?'

'Give me time to get organized, Francis!'

For three years, while Nigel grew out of the need for Free Dinners and out of trousers far too long for him, Mr Bluett kept a distant, caring eye on the first black rabbit to enter the Adelaide Bing hutch, pleading with Mr Coote not to confiscate his football quite so often, challenging Miss Oates whenever she left him standing outside her class-room door . . .

And now Nigel was ten—and his to shape and mould. He had cherished the prospect of this winter, the commencement of a partnership to prove that a boy who fights harder than the rest can win the greater victories. Why not Nigel as Commonwealth Secretary or Commanding Officer of a British regiment? Hadn't his white compeers by their sceptical attitudes and crass behaviour betrayed the heritage bequeathed to them?

'Only *Nigel* knows his tables!', 'Look at *Nigel's* painting!', 'Watch how *Nigel* heads the ball!'

Such praise was intended to offset the girls' dislike of touching the boy or being near him. At start of term, one had made her revulsion plain.

'Lorraine, you're late! Go and sit by Nigel!'

She queried the command by halting in her tracks.

'Yes, go and sit by Nigel!'

'I'm not late, sir. You ain't called the Register.'

'It's not a punishment! There's no other desk free—'

'Catch me beside a wog!'

The wounded Nigel, arms in pouncing posture, simulated Dracula to pretend he didn't care.

'What was that?'

No answer. She must know she had done wrong.

'What did you say?'

A sullen silence.

'I want to hear what you called Nigel.'

Still Lorraine dared not utter.

'I want you to repeat what you said about Nigel. It's something we'd better discuss. Not just you and I. All of us. Nigel included.'

'I called him a wog, sir.'

'And what does "wog" mean?'

'Don't know, sir. Golliwog, I suppose.'

'It means a Westernized Oriental Gentleman. Tell Lorraine where you're from, Nigel!'

'Magnolia Court, sir.'

'No, where you were born!'

'Bart's Hospital, sir.'

The rest of the class were growing restless. Lorraine relaxed.

'Don't you understand, boy? Where's your father from?'

'My father's dead, sir!'

'I'm sorry. I should have remembered. Miss Hodge told me . . . No, what I meant was, "What country did your father originally come from?"!'

'From Ghana, sir.'

'Did you hear that, Lorraine? Ghana! Not the Orient!'

'There's somebody wants you at the door!' a boy shouted from the back.

'Well ask him to come in!'

'It's a she.'

'Well ask *her* to come in!'

'Come in!', 'Come in!' they yelled.

'Miss Hodge is waiting to begin Assembly.'

'Tell Miss Hodge I'll hold mine in my room . . . Now then, Lorraine, show me Ghana on the map!'

She put her finger on Singapore.

'No, Lorraine. If Nigel's father came from there, you might have had an excuse if not a reason for calling him what you did— but "wog" usually applies, and not very politely, to Indians of India *here*. Nigel's father, however, came from over here— Africa. And is Africa oriental?'

'Yes, sir.'

'It is not! Define "oriental"!'

'Can't, sir.'

'It means "eastern". Now, is Ghana eastern?'

'Yes, sir . . . I mean No, sir.'

'It's south-western, isn't it? It would have been more accurate to call Nigel a Westernized Occidental . . .' He paused. The initials had not changed. '. . . a Westernized Occidental Gentleman, which is nonsense. Understood? You may now go to your place, Lorraine.'

'I don't want to sit beside Nigel, sir.'

'Go to your place!'

'There's someone at the door!' a boy shouted.

'Well tell her to come in!'

'It's a he!'

Laughter.

'Miss Walsh is waiting for the Dinner Money.'

'Of all the inopportune . . . Get out!'

'She said not to leave till you handed it to me, sir.'

'Get out!' bellowed Mr Bluett, and the boy disappeared.

One was hampered by pettiness at Adelaide Bing! There was never a chance to come to grips with the wider issues!

'Lorraine, do what I'm asking or you'll be sorry!'

'No!'

'Yes, Lorraine.'

'No!'

'Yes!'

This last was Nigel's.

'From Nigel least of all do I expect insolence!'

'I didn't mind her calling me "wog", sir. Usually she calls me "The Ape"!'

' "The Ape"?'

'Ape!', 'Ape!' everyone cried, and Nigel beat his chest and scratched his armpits.

'Silence!'

'Ape!', 'Ape!' . . .

Lorraine was nearest. Mr Bluett struck her across the face.

'Once and for all, go sit where you've been told!'

She sobbed and pressed her knuckles to her cheek and would not budge. He lifted her bodily to Nigel's desk and flung her down.

'Sit there and like it, you little hussy!'

Snivelling, head in arms upon the desk-lid, she waited till his back was turned.

'Wait till me Dad gets on to yer!' she screamed. 'He'll knock yer balls off, yer fuckin' bastard!'

'Perhaps I have been expecting too much of a girl who speaks that kind of language. Please remember all of you, not just Lorraine, that "the head and the hoof of the Law and the haunch and the hip is—Obey!" Nigel, collect Dinner Money! Line up those who are staying!'

The headmistress sent for Mr Bluett during playtime.

'Why didn't you bring your class to Assembly this morning?'

'Lorraine wouldn't sit beside Nigel. It was worth discussing while passions were running high.'

'The very time *not* to hold a discussion, I'd have thought.'

'We got things out of our systems. Cleared the air.'

'I do hope you're not going to favour Nigel at the expense of the rest. If he realizes you're prepared to cut my assemblies on his account . . .'

'I'd cut a dozen if it would teach the others not to call him "Ape"! The poor boy has to pretend to *like* it!'

'Whether he likes it or not, I'd rather you didn't cut Assembly again. Especially at the start of another academic year . . .'

'Academic! The Inspectors deny us the right to speak of nouns and adverbs . . .'

'Forgive me interrupting, but there's something else. Miss Walsh has been upset. Apparently you dismissed a messenger of hers extremely curtly and were late with your Dinner Money.'

'Women!'

'You never had much time for us, did you, Francis?'

'Never?' The injustice riled him. 'I've got to go. The bell is ringing.'

He poured some brandy into his coffee and took it to the classroom.

'Handwriting test. A sheet of this paper each, Nigel! Name and date top right hand side, everyone. Begin when you're ready. Copy from the board. A sheet *each*, Nigel! Are you deaf? Here! On my table!'

He was glad of any opportunity to fault the boy. Appearing to treat him as a favourite would harm the cause.

'Oh, East is East, and West is West, and never the twain
shall meet,
Till Earth and Sky stand presently at God's great
Judgment Seat;—'

'Sir! Sir! Sir!'

'Yes, whoever you are.'

'We're not supposed to use capitals except for names and at the start of a sentence.'

'Quite right, but Rudyard Kipling was important enough to be allowed to break the rules.'

'Unfair!'

Mr Bluett continued writing.

'But there is neither East nor West, Border, nor Breed,
nor Birth,
When two strong men stand face to face, though they
come from the ends of the earth!'

'Now then, those that are finished, which words in this famous verse rhyme?'

' "Meet" and "bum", I mean "Seat", sir.'

'Who said that?'

No answer.

'There's a coward in our midst. I'll repeat my question. Who said "bum"?'

'Nigel did, sir!' Lorraine giggled.

'I'll see you later, you female Judas! Is this true, Nigel?'

'Yes, sir.'

'And do you think you impress? Do you think it's a credit to your race to speak with the vulgarity of your white compatriots? What would your mother say?'

'She'd say "arse", sir.'

His face was an impenetrable cloud. Was he buying popularity? Had he missed the meaning of the question? Was he stupid? Was he subtle? Was he hinting at his mother's deficiencies? Was it true that she neglected his moral well-being?

The class hooted and fell about. How best to restore order? He banged his fist on the blackboard.

A messenger came for Lorraine during Maths next afternoon— meaning her parents had arrived to accuse Mr Bluett of violence.

He tried to concentrate on what he was expounding.

'Anything to the right of the point is less than one, less than a whole. It's a piece, a part, a share. The point, in other words, is a barrier. To the left of it stand units, tens, hundreds, thousands. To the right of it we have our less than ones—our tenths, hundredths . . .'

For all their bits of squared paper cut into varying lengths, Lizzie Oates and Colin Coote had failed to impart the meaning of a decimal.

The messenger returned.

'I shall be gone for quite some time. Anyone talking or out of his place when I get back will be severely punished. Make up a number containing a decimal point, and set a value on each of the digits. Then read your library books.'

He took a nip of brandy on the stairs.

'Shake you by the 'and!' scoffed Lorraine's Mum when he said, 'How do you do!'

'The feckin' 'and that struck my daughter!' dittoed Dad, his fists clenched white.

He knew that Muriel would be no help. She believed in nothing. She was committed to nothing. She would steer the middle course that obtained her her promotion. All parties would leave her study—her 'power-house' as she cared to call it—semi-satisfied and cheated of their intentions. No principle would triumph. Adelaide Bing would continue marking time in the circular direction of nowhere.

'Sit down, Mr Bluett. I'm sure you've already guessed the reason for this interview. Lorraine has stated her complaint. Now let's hear yours.'

'Lorraine arrived late. She refused to sit where she was told. Only one space was available . . .'

'So you struck 'er! You struck our daughter!'

'Not, Madam, till after she had called the partner to whom she objected a "wog" and an "ape"!'

'This ain't true, is it Lorraine?'

Seeing Dad relent, Mum took possession of the cudgels. 'So you punished her, did you, for speaking her mind? Girls shouldn't have to sit beside boys. It puts them off their work.'

'This is a co-educational school. You knew that when Lorraine came here. Can't you see Mr Bluett's predicament?'

'Miss Hodge, there is no predicament!' interrupted Mr Bluett angrily. 'Lorraine was in the wrong. She disobeyed her teacher and groundlessly affronted a fellow-pupil. It was left to me to settle the matter. I did so. My method was a last resort.'

'It weren't just me!'

'You started the ball rolling, young lassie!'

'You asked me why I didn't want to sit beside Nigel!'

'Lorraine has a point there, Mr Bluett. She told you a truth you demanded of her in public.'

'She couched that truth in unnecessarily cruel terms, Miss Hodge!'

'Quite so, but should we punish her for a weak vocabulary?'

Mum and Dad exchanged smug looks.

'Surely Lorraine can sit beside a friend of her own choice?' said Dad.

'No! Lorraine must sit beside Nigel!'

'But why, Mr Bluett!'

'Miss Hodge! Quite apart from the loss to my authority, if Lorraine here offends Nigel in a permanent way by . . .'

'Is this Nigel a bleedin' pouffe? Everything seems to offend the little bastard! 'Asn't 'e a mind of 'is own? Can't we 'ear 'is side of it, Miss 'Odge?'

'An excellent idea. I was about to make the same suggestion. Lorraine! You heard your father? Run and fetch Nigel, there's a good girl!'

Trust Muriel! Not even to defend her most loyal member of staff would she forgo the expedient of asking children to resolve their own problems, problems of whose complexity they could have no comprehension.

While the parents continued to defend their daughter—'She's ever so 'elpful in the 'ome!', 'She enjoyed school ever so much until this year!'—Mr Bluett looked about the room. Frilly net curtains! Ugh! How insipid Muriel had become over the years!

'Don't be shy!' she was saying.

Nigel looked shifty. 'Head up, boy! Straighten those shoulders! Choose which one of us to stare in the eye!' Mr Bluett wanted to advise.

'What's the trouble, sonny? I'm Lorraine's Dad. Did she insult you?'

Yes, yes, man! Speak up! Where's your pride? Surely the cause is worthy of some present suffering?!

'Well, Nigel?' coaxed Miss Hodge.

'What did our daughter do to you? For Christ's sake wag your tongue! Me and my 'usband's late back for work already!'

'She called me "The Ape".'

'What everyone else calls you?' Lorraine had told her of Nigel's nickname.

'Yes.'

Mr Bluett flushed annoyance. 'She also called him a "wog". Do you mean to say, Nigel, that you really don't mind being called a "wog" and an "ape"?!'

'No, sir. It's only in fun.'

'And you don't mind Lorraine refusing to sit beside you, either?'

'No, sir.'

Whereupon Lorraine's Dad threatened Mr Bluett with a prosecution should he ever so much as lay a finger on his 'baby' again, and Lorraine, after promising Miss Hodge to continue to be a good girl, was sent back to her classroom along with Nigel.

Mr Bluett later found the pair of them working contentedly together at the same desk. 'Lorraine has no close friends,' he explained to Muriel afterwards. 'No one but Nigel particularly wants to sit with her.'

'Then we'll have to install another desk.'

Nigel and Lorraine became the only members of Mr Bluett's class to sit alone in a room already short of space.

'Nigel' cropped up a week later in the staff-room.

Lady Sandra was embroidering a reticule, a therapy employed to forget the seven-year-olds who spat at her on first acquaintance.

Colin Coote was passing on riddles to Lizzie Oates:

'What's brown and mad?'

'No idea.'

'A nut!'

He gleefully exercised his toes and ankles, and probed between the thighs of his denim flares with Art-loving fingers. To be asked riddles demonstrated how popular he was, how quickly he could break down barriers and reach an easy intimacy with his pupils.

'And what is black and white and red all over?'

'Everyone knows that one! A newspaper!'

'No! An embarrassed zebra!'

Lizzie had a marking pencil behind each ear and was dressed like a Victorian baker's boy. Groaning loudly, she leaped towards the gas oven.

'Anyone for slosh?'

Lady Sandra smiled towards Mr Bluett. At moments such as these he found it comforting to have an ally staunchly pitted against the loud and vulgar.

'Yes, I'd love a cup of tea, my dear. My cup's the green one.'

Miss Oates winked at Mr Coote. She, on her side, found it

116

comforting to have a confederate with whom to fight the forces of reaction.

'Same for you, Mr Bluett?'

'No, thanks. I'll deal with my own.'

'Col?'

'Ta, love! The usual.'

'Ta, love!!' To such verbal coarseness could be ascribed his success with the Inspectorate whose notion it was to side with the children and never to uplift them!

Conversation turned inevitably to Schoolkeeper's Grumbles.

'While we're together, the Fuehrer's moaning again!' Though Coote mocked the schoolkeeper—it was he who dubbed him 'Fuehrer'—no one more willingly relayed his dictates. 'Since the introduction of paper towels, there have not been enough items for the School laundry parcel, so would you all please hand in your blackboard-cloths for washing at the end of every week. Second, the cleaner is on Time and Motion—she has approximately three minutes per classroom—so would you all remember that one chair not put on its desk at night considerably hinders her efficiency. Third, a new girl, one of Lady Sandra's, has been asked to take down her knickers in the brush cupboard. By whom she will not say. The Fuehrer thinks it was Nigel.'

'I resent that allegation!'

'Mr Bluett, I'm only repeating what the Fuehrer told me!'

'Nigel, if we're not very careful, will become the scapegoat for all that's nasty in this school.'

'But if it were true . . .'

'Lady Sandra! I'm surprised!'

'The girl did say the boy was big and black. As he's the oldest and the worst of them we've got . . .'

'She was probably put up to it! Look, let's have this out once and for all! Is there anything special about Nigel apart from his colour? I've the right to know. This is a crucial year so far as he's concerned. The type of school he goes to will largely depend on the profile I write of him.'

'You must judge him for yourself, Mr Bluett.'

'That, Mr Coote, I certainly shall. But it would greatly assist me towards that end if I heard how each of the rest of you have found him. I've already had one incident this term. Now with the Fuehrer on the warpath . . .'

'Oh, forget Nigel for once, and pour yourself some tea!'

'I'm not going to have this boy victimized, Miss Oates! Tell me, Lady Sandra! Teething troubles apart, was Nigel a nuisance to you?'

'He fed a terrapin to the gerbils.'

'Miss Oates?'

'He spent most of the year outside my door.'

'Mr Coote?'

' "When in doubt, ignore"! *I* never bothered Nigel, except to confiscate his football, so Nigel decided not to bother *me*!'

Mr Bluett walked out of the room carrying his tea-mug. With tears in his eyes, he hurried down to the playground where he was supposed to be on duty.

He strolled over to where, in a corner by himself, Nigel was morosely playing with a football.

'Don't worry, Nigel! We're going to fight this thing together.'

'What thing, sir?'

'And keep on practising! I want you for the team . . . Hey you! Over there! Yes, you, Gary. Come over here a moment! Why isn't Nigel in your game?'

'Doesn't want to be, sir.'

'True or false, Nigel?'

'True, sir.'

'He never lends his ball, sir!'

'They play with it after the whistle and the teacher on duty takes it!'

'An intolerable dilemma. Thank you, Gary. Thank you, Nigel. You may both go now.'

Nigel must be saved.

At a cost of leprosy, yaws, sleeping sickness, malaria; at a cost of life itself, the Motherland had accepted into her hands a Negro baby. And for what? To allow it grow to be a lad who was afraid to share his football in a back-street yard? For *this* was an empire surrendered and a Commonwealth created?!

The patience of the swimming instructor was said to be inexhaustible, but he said, 'That Negro boy, he's yours this year? Don't bother bringing him! I suppose with that flailing motion he hopes to frighten away the crocodiles. Look how the dirt shows white on him! Water's a God they won't abuse by washing!'

Mr Bluett's intentions hardened. He would make a hero of Nigel, a paragon whose physique, whose brain, whose strength of character would put his pigmy foes to shame. He did not care when a student-trainee was foisted on him temporarily by Muriel. He abandoned the majority to concocting silly seed mosaics and, on the pretext of punishing Nigel for insolence, removed him to the library for special coaching. He taught him the meaning of 'onomatopoeia', 'simile' and $2\pi r$. He explained the Stock Exchange, and how to write a cheque. He lent him the latest edition of 'Wisden'. He showed him the 'Kennedy's Latin Primer' he used himself at school.

'I suppose you miss your other teachers.'

'Yes, sir. Except for Lady Sandra. Wish we didn't have her still for Nature. Lady Sandra's a wet!'

'She's a very remarkable person, Nigel. She doesn't have to teach. She's very rich.'

'You should hear her try to imitate a chiff-chaff— dadddddddd*dd*de!'

'That'll be enough, Nigel!'

He was glad, though, that the boy poked fun at her. Her attitude to discipline made her a classic example of what Kipling used to call 'the sinner-who-faces-both-ways'.

'Mr Coote never took you for football, did he?'

'No, sir. But Mr Coote's OK.'

'*I*'ve decided to make you Centre Half on the school team!'

'Gee, sir! Thanks! Who do you support?'

'I support Adelaide Bing.'

Mr Bluett detested the game. On the other hand, till cricket in the summer term, it was a means of spending the energy of his most troublesome boys. His advice never to be selfish but to pass—or was it his lemons at half-time?—had embedded Adelaide Bing at the bottom of the local League.

'Miss Oates supports Aston Villa!'

'A jolly good teacher, Miss Oates!'

The hoped-for contradiction never came.

'Yeah! Almost as good as Mr Coote. We had fun with her and Mr Coote!'

'Is there anything you like apart from football, Nigel?'

'Mucking about, sir.'

If Livingstone and Rhodes could hear this news! Scions nurtured so that one day they, too, should blossom petals of the rose, all stultified and withered through lack of regular watering! Was the purpose of railways, medicine, forestry, roads, canals, law courts, civil service, army, schools, to enable Nigel and his kind to *muck about*?!

'But you must have a hobby! Do you read?'

'No, sir.'

'Are you a scout?'

'No, sir.'

'Do you go to church?'

'No, sir.'

Did he fish, play cricket, make models, explore museums? No! The boy might as well be in the jungle under an ebony tree chewing kola-nut!

'How much pocket-money do you get?'

'None, sir.'

'You help your mother as you ought?'

'Yes, sir.'

'Have you a bicycle?'

'No, sir.'

'Do you collect stamps?'

'No, sir.'

'Would you *like* to collect stamps?'

Nigel was eager for deliverance.

'Oh yes, sir!'

Next day, Mr Bluett presented him with a Stanley Gibbon's album, a packet of hinges, a magnifying glass, a pair of tweezers and a mixed bag of stamps from his own Commonwealth collection.

'I regret that Ghanaian stamps are now discredited. Maybe the likes of you, Nigel, will one day rehabilitate them.'

An evangelist at the exit to Earl's Court station handed Mr Bluett a religious tract.

'The Lord loves you,' he said, 'and wants to enter your heart and forgive you your sins.'

'Am I so obviously drunk?'

'God bless you! Only by Love can Good be defended and Evil overcome!'

The loneliness he must endure this Christmas fortnight more befitted Lent than the Nativity. No longer was it 'Should I have sacrificed my teaching life to Muriel?' The problem to be faced was 'Why teach at all if Nigel won't respond?'

Glass in hand, he mooned in semi-slumber beside the stove of his bed-sitter.

'The clay is moist and soft. Now, now, make haste and form the pitcher on the rapid wheel!' At boarding school a master could fashion, ornament, erase from dawn till nightfall. Yet how could a Nigel ever afford the treatment he most needed?

Season of goodwill! He looked at the mantelpiece. A man over fifty, a man of his background, and only a motto-calendar there, given by the man at the Dry Cleaner's! In his briefcase were some unspeakable cards and an unspeakable pair of brass cuff-links from a handful of unspeakable children, but from Nigel he had received nothing! Nigel was a monstrous ingrate, and the thought was plaguing him.

Lunch hour after lunch hour after lunch hour, he had been prepared to grind the boy for his first Intelligence Test in November. 'We don't want you fit to be nothing but a road-sweeper, do we?'

'Complete the next two items of this series:
O,T,T,F,F, . . .'

'Here is a word in which the letters are arranged in alpha-betical order instead of the usual way. Write the proper word:
ABCELNOST'

'If you were rich are you sure you would be happy?
Yes. No. I do not know.
Underline the correct answer.'

Lizzie Oates was suspicious.

'The sportsmaster of Hawksworth for you on the phone . . . Hello! What's this? Have I interrupted a tête-à-tête? . . . Oh, I see! A spot of private coaching!'

'Rubbish! This is punishment pure and simple.'

'You do understand, Mr Bluett, that under Rule Four of our Union's "Code of Conduct" it is considered unprofessional for any teacher systematically to detain scholars in primary schools for extra tuition?'

'I do not belong to any Union, Miss Oates.' It should be the policy of her Union to assist the Nigels of this world, not to neglect them. The racial prejudice of adults was infecting the children. No youngster could have invented their riddles and their jingles!

> 'One banana, two banana, three banana, four;
> One little Paki lying on the floor.
> Along came a skinhead,
> Kicked him in the head.
> Now another Paki's lying down dead.'

'Oh, stop that, Gary! The Pakistanis have been very good friends to you and me.'

'What would you call a black man with a machine-gun?'

'I've no idea, Lorraine.'

'You'd call 'im "sir"!'

'Hardly very funny!'

'Don't you get it? A black man with a machine-gun. You'd call 'im "sir" to stop 'im killing you!'

'But why a *black* man, Lorraine? I'd call anybody "sir" who threatened me! . . .'

If only this Christmas it had been possible to kidnap Nigel, snatch him from the hot-house, smother-love of home and give him a happy and instructive time—the Queen's Message; reading from 'The Jungle Book' and 'King Solomon's Mines'; visits to Madame Tussaud's and 'Peter Pan'; brisk walking in Regent's Park; Monopoly!

The recent Coote-Oates Nativity accurately represented the shabby tone Adelaide Bing had sunk to. 'See yer!' shouted Joseph as he drove away to find himself a job, leaving Mary in a garage playing flower-pot chime bars till a doll fell out of her miniskirt and three Arsenal players who had followed the light of the GPO Tower knocked on the door and offered gifts of cornflakes, cigarettes and washing-up liquid.

Nigel, at the all-day party, instead of withstanding the excesses Britain was affording him, evinced as much pleasure as the two-a-penny white boys at his elbow.

'Lovely to see kids happy!' cried Coote to Oates without a trace of irony as staff distributed more orange juice and ices in answer to the chant of 'We want more!'

Mr Bluett stayed the arm of Lady Sandra.

'Wait till they've quietened!'

'Oh let's overlook it! Let's give them fun!'

'A lazy way out!'

He shouted for silence.

'If these infernal bad manners continue, I shall refuse to show films afterwards!'

Sandwich crusts and bun-cases began to fly.

Miss Hodge was sitting in her study, staring vacantly at her frilly curtains.

'Muriel, how can you remain here when the children are behaving like animals in the hall?'

'*I* can't hear them!'

'You don't want to hear them!'

'Francis, go away! I have matters of policy to attend to!'

'Policy? What policy! Adelaide Bing is a free for all!'

'Please go away!'

The number of occasions when she could gather strength enough to handle Francis was increasing.

'I only mean to help you, Muriel!'

'Well do so by showing the films and leaving me alone!'

Mr Bluett was amazed. She used to be so shy.

The films were pre-sound.

Those who could read yelled the sub-titles in unison:

'TODAY IS THE CASHIER'S BIRTHDAY. THIRTY AND STILL COMES HOME AT ANY TIME HE LIKES!'

He shouldn't have been candid with Muriel . . .

'FAILING TO GET THE POLICE ON THE PHONE CHARLIE SENT THEM A POSTCARD—'

'Shut up! . . . Very well then!'—he flicked the projector to a standstill. 'Lights!'

Respectful, blink-eyed faces were peering towards him.

'That will be all. Lead out from the front!'

Someone, somewhere, had to draw the line. Why didn't Deputy Coote as Master of Ceremonies curb the gluttony at tea or, for that matter, put a stop to the whistles and cat-calls yesterday at the Fancy Dress Parade?

Thoughts of the Fancy Dress Parade rankled above all else. He had meant Nigel to win.

'I've hired you this costume from Berman's.'

'What am I?'

'Othello.'

The boy's eyes glittered. The most frightening Bluebeard, the prettiest Harlequin, the funniest St Trinian, the toughest Hell's Angel, the most ingenious Letter-Box, Torch or Christmas Pudding couldn't possibly outclass him.

'What's a "thello"?'

'A warrior and a nobleman. What did you go as last year?'

'A coal-hole.'

Mr Bluett remembered.

'And the year before that, with Miss Oates?'

'A bottle of ink.'

'And with Lady Sandra?'

'A scare-crow.'

'This year you shall be a prince.'

Nigel touched the chain-mail of the tunic, then the scabbard whose inlaid precious stones he believed in these blazing moments to be real.

'Can I try it on?'

Mr Bluett locked the classroom door and put a blackboard against it.

'Only ten minutes till the end of play. Quick! Shirt and trousers off!'

The beauty of the boy surpassed Tiepolo's 'Moor'.

'Fine! Absolutely splendid! Now, look sharp! Into the box! Let's keep it hidden in my cupboard!'

The matter of the costume had been discussed this evening at the staff's Christmas get-together.

'Ah! The very bloke we've been waiting for! Mateus Rosé or Bristol Cream, Mr Bluett?'

'Sherry, thank you, Mr Coote.'

'I was telling the rest that when the Football Captain showed up at the Fancy Dress Parade as "A Fella" I said, "Gary, no one I'm sure has ever doubted you were anything else!" It took me several moments to grasp he meant "Othello"!'

'The costume was Nigel's. Gary persuaded him to part with it.'

'You mean the costume was yours and, because of that, Nigel decided not to wear it.'

'You didn't have to hand him a mop and send him down the aisle as a chimney-sweep!'

'Aren't you being over-sensitive?'

Lizzie Oates supported him. 'Colin had only a split second in which to think!'

'Nobleman to chimney-sweep was the reverse of the process I had in mind.'

Muriel was ahemming.

'Time, perhaps, to begin my speech . . . This year I don't intend to ration praise . . .'

Mr Bluett asked Colin Coote to refill his glass. Coote shook an empty bottle :

'Sorry, old chap!' he mimicked. 'You'll have to make do with your own supplies.'

Lady Sandra, hoping by a torrent of words to take the sting from this impudence, indulged in an animated flight of fancy whose irrelevance served to underline Mr Coote's aberration and to put Miss Hodge out of oratorical step :

'How does a non-amphibian come to exist on a desert island? How about that for an opener next term, Mr Bluett? That should grab them, as they say!'

'May I grab you?' Miss Hodge requested.

The young ones seemed to share some licentious notion, and there was an interval of restless embarrassment while all attempted to re-focus on their headmistress and the prospect of her pronouncements.

'No captain could be prouder of her crew than I am. Though manacled to my desk by bureaucracy's thousand and one demands, I have again justifiably remained confident that the rest of you could cope with the Christmas chores and win through without a hitch. Thank you, Mr Coote, our boatswain, under whose capable guidance Adelaide Bing has again evaded both Scylla and Charybdis. Thank you all hands. Thank you. Thank you. Bottoms up and down the hatch!'

There was a flurry of raised elbows and of false denials and reciprocated, tiddly compliments. But Miss Hodge hadn't finished.

'Never has there been quite such a lovely show of reindeer, Santas, bells, angels, cribs, Stars in the East, camels and Wise Men—though I'm hard put as ever to guess why Mr Bluett hasn't provided us with anything, not even a Melchior!'

'I prefer modesty to display.'

'When it suits!' objected the Deputy. 'Don't forget your Historical Wall Picture of "The Death of Wolfe Before Quebec"! *And* your Commonwealth Map!'

Miss Hodge was simpering on regardless:

'. . . Schoolkeeper, Secretary, cleaner, dinner ladies—all thank you for your generous gifts, and may I say personally what a wonderful idea it was of Mr Coote's to purchase them out of tea-money profits! . . . And that is all, I think, except to wish each one of you a very merry . . .'

There was a loud knock at the door.

Coote pranced over, opened it a fraction and remained in secretive confabulation.

'Come on! Let's see who it is!' cried Lady Sandra, skittishly clinking one of her three diamond rings against the rim of her glass.

'We're not lepers!' agreed Lizzie Oates.

'As you wish!'—and Coote swung the door wide with a shrug of his effeminate shoulders.

'Nigel!!' Mr Bluett was on his feet. 'Not gone yet?!'

'I forgot these, sir.'

Coy as a lover with a posy, he produced a pile of envelopes from behind his back.

'What are they? Christmas cards from you! Oh, I say! This is charming! What a very, very thoughtful and polite young man! One for Miss Hodge. One for you as well, Miss Oates. Mr Coote. Lady Sandra. Miss Walsh—she isn't here. We'll post hers on . . .'

'I've got a cocker spaniel. Isn't he perfectly sweet! All decked out in a paper hat and playing a piano!'

'Mine's got Father Christmas on an elephant!'

'Mine's a stained-glass window!'

'Mine's a jeep!'

'Thank you!'

'Yes, thanks a lot, Nigel!'

'You drew them all yourself?'

'Our clever little King of Nubia!'

None of them yet realized that Mr Bluett had received nothing.

Despite everything, Mr Bluett husbanded his faith. Soil and climate must be indifferent, not the grain.

'How did you spend Christmas, Nigel?'

'Watched telly.'

'Now it is January,' recurred Muriel, 'the first month of the year. With one of his faces Janus looks back upon the old. With the other he looks forward to the new. Hands up those children who have made New Year resolutions! . . . No one. Hands up those who are prepared to make them now!'

'Not to break the chairs', 'Not to stuff soap up the taps' . . .

While we're at it, Muriel, why not ask for resolutions from your staff? Colin Coote might promise not to make sly trunk-calls at the school's expense. Lady Sandra might sweep the maggots and dead bluebottles from her cages. Lizzie Oates might extinguish her classroom lights at break-times.

In proportion as his plan to advance Nigel grew more determined, the more exasperating were the fallibilities of those who appeared to be obstructing it. He entered the staff-room one morning to find his keys on the wrong ring, and hamster food, batteries and a milk-top tambourine on the shelf reserved for his bowler hat.

'Good morning, Mr Bluett!'

Lady Sandra was the only member of the trio ever to acknowledge his arrival.

'Good morning to *you*, Lady Sandra!'

'I am under attack from Miss Oates for having told a child . . .'

'Yes, as science mistress—'

'Since when?'

'Oh belt up, Colin! Science was my main subject!'

'What's electricity, then?'

'Nobody knows. As I was saying, *before* I was so rudely interrupted . . .' Here she cast a frown at Coote who crumpled up in merriment murmuring, 'What a girl! What a girl!' '. . . As science mistress, I strongly object to Lady Sandra telling a boy that slugs can talk!'

'Children are so tiny when they come to me.'

'Size is no excuse for telling lies.'

'I'm sure slugs communicate.'

'Perhaps so, Lady Sandra. But you told a boy they *talk*! Not only that, you said they sing!!'

'Marvellous!' Coote clapped his hands delightedly. 'My class will perform a Slug Opera this week! Tinkling triangles in the background to suggest silvery trails!'

'Down with phantasy! Up with fact!' pursued Lizzie Oates.

'So you propose no more Jemima Puddleduck? No more Toad of Toad Hall?' Lady Sandra was unrepentant. 'No more Father Christmas?'

'Exactly! And no more Queen and Commonwealth from Mr Bluett, either. Brainwashing defenceless children! It turns my stomach!'

For none of them, save Mr Bluett, was this typical debate more than a diversion. Only Mr Bluett afterwards continued to worry over pros and cons. With no curriculum, with each new teacher a law unto himself, where was the school going? Why was it left to him to sort the muddle, weave the strands, raise the top-year children to examination standard, give them the chance in life they neither knew nor cared was there? Was it honourable this year to be helping Nigel only? Yet he had given half his life, hadn't he, to the white children of the Commonwealth and they had abused the privilege?

'Why do you bully Nigel?' Lorraine had asked.

He congratulated himself on the deception. Nigel, indeed, believed to be his teacher's foe, was achieving popularity. No more skulking in the playground with his football. He was always in the fray. He and Gary, the Football King, were thick as thieves. During Saturday League Matches in the local park, they shared crude jokes about their sponsor. Mr Bluett knew this, tolerated the ingratitude. Nigel was weaned. What was his own personal sacrifice compared with the emergence and integration of oppressed Commonwealth peoples everywhere?! As the ragged team moiled to and from the pitch, it was Nigel whom Mr Bluett checked for crossing a road without permission, Nigel whom he ordered from a sweetshop, Nigel whom he censured for bad language. The rest might do as they pleased. Let passers-by frown, tut-tut, halt in their tracks to stare in mock astonishment—Mr Bluett wasn't bothered. The end justified the means. In the classroom where, say, Gary or Lorraine's compositions received a hasty tick, Nigel's were combed for every error. In PE Nigel, not the rest, had to repeat each exercise to perfection. In Maths it was Nigel who was asked to practise long multiplication and long division, and to estimate the distance he walked to school and the amount of milk he drank per annum.

'Obviously avenging Nigel's behaviour last term!'—staff and children were entitled to their thoughts. His conscience was clear. His motives were pure. Nigel might hate him now. One day the boy would understand his obligation, shed tears of gratitude and not self-pity. Hadn't strictness already brought about the rising of his star? Didn't boys and girls now deign to speak to him, slaves, as it were, united in a common hatred of their driver?

While frost still lichened the morning pavements of February, Miss Hodge demanded elaborate reports on all Mr Bluett's pupils so she could choose them new schools for the autumn. He had to apply himself, therefore, to inventing a personality for Nigel that would pass muster and ensure him decent prospects though he had bungled each of his examinations.

He knocked on the Secretary's door.

'May I have this year's profile sheets, Miss Walsh? How quickly the task has come round again! And may I have the records made by my colleagues, too?'

'I thought you always came to your own conclusions, Mr Bluett.'

'I can't see what business it is of yours!'

She hastened to the filing cabinet. He regretted his abruptness. He apologized with an inexactitude:

'Forgive me! A flu cold!'

'Yes, you don't look well. You don't look well at all!'

Regretting his apology, he examined his face in the staff-room mirror.

'What's she on about, damned female!'

He fortified himself with today's fifth alcoholic nip, before slipping Nigel's folder into his briefcase. Not till he was thrumming along the District Line at home-time was he able to peruse its contents.

General Personality Sketch : 'Unco-operative and vicious. Teases the animals. Breaks the flowers.'

Vicious at the age of eight? Isn't that too strong, Lady Sandra, too summary? Naughty, perhaps. Boys will be boys. Isn't it rather you who are vicious for choosing such an epithet? You can sound so sweet, so gentle! Yet did you take the trouble to observe and sympathize with Nigel as you do with your livestock? How can you expect a high-rise flat-dweller to care about the flora and fauna of your Blackheath habitat? You remind me of those out-of-touch dance hostesses I partnered in country halls when I served in the Beach Brigade of the Royal Norfolks!

Particular Abilities and Interests : 'Neat handwriting.'

Nothing else? What about his spelling? I've found it exceptionally good. What of his drawing? What of his athleticism? Ah, I forget! Games and Physical Education you ignore. Your nurture of growing things stops short at human beings!

Special Needs : 'The cane.'

My oh my! Given the official attitude towards corporal punishment we *are* confident of our invulnerable position, aren't we? Because we are the daughter of a marquis we are entitled to air any independent view!

Language : 'Unimaginative.'

Wasn't prepared to believe slugs sing, I suppose. Did you build on what you learned about the boy—his Ghanaian origins, his love of stamps and football? Did you ever try him on the tropics instead of on that blasted heath of yours?

Maths : 'Can repeat his tables.'

How patronizing! Why not 'has learned' or 'knows' his tables? Still the professional do-gooder, Lady Sandra! You *deserve* it when the children scratch the enamel off your Armstrong Siddeley! All you offer lifts to are your caged creatures and your flowers. Your car is like a hearse. Your remote brand of charity is as damaging as Miss Oates' and Mr Coote's misguided self-indulgence.

How had *they* stereotyped Nigel? First Miss Oates.

'Big for his age.'

Poor Lizzie! What a typically feminine niminy-piminy reaction! Maybe you fear him!

'The girls object to his pulling their hair and worse.'

Sarcastic. Condemnatory. Here on the record you write it for everybody connected with his education to read till he reaches puberty and beyond. This bewitching Sambo is a threat to your own maidenhead, isn't he—assuming yours is still intact?

'Nigel is sullen, selfish and moody. Tampers with science experiments of cleverer children out of jealousy and spite.'

Not, of course, out of healthy curiosity!

'Unconstructive. Cannot be lured into purposeful activity. Breaks cantilevers, spring-balances and pendulums, and, when there is no equipment left to wreck in my Resource Areas, resorts to tearing the wings off common house-flies.'

The disease is catching. Picked up from Lady Sandra, it will next contaminate Coote and could have spread with the years. Fortunately I am here to arrest its progress.

'Though Nigel reads well, his written stories show no signs of giftedness. Our visits to the Science Museum and Greenwich Observatory were not recorded in his diary. . . . He is mathematically lost. Venn diagrams, topology, and core and environmental numeracy confuse him. Can't handle Dienes' Apparatus or Cuisenaire Rods. Won't play polyominoes.'

Well, you enjoyed writing that, didn't you, Miss Oates? But you make no mention of his special needs, nor, I note, of his 'giftedness' as an athlete. All this has been a veiled excuse, hasn't it, to advertise your trendiness and showcase methods?

Mr Bluett had to brace himself with brandy before reading the observations of Mr Coote.

'I wouldn't mind a drop of that meself!' joked an Irishman sitting opposite.

Mr Bluett loathed Colin Coote. His loathing was instinctive—like that of a dog which growls at cats, whose mere cattiness sends danger signals up and down its spine. The loathing was mutual, and Coote adequately defended himself with bumptious repartee.

Mr Bluett would eventually be driven from the room, while the other stayed his ground to chatter on with either Lizzie, who admired his nerve, or Lady Sandra who endured him as part payment towards her advantages of birth. If it hurt Mr Bluett to watch Miss Oates hold her knife between thumb and forefinger, it racked him to watch Coote do the same. Though it seemed natural for Miss Oates to string pendants and love-beads around her neck, on Coote they looked offensive. Long hair on Miss Oates looked lovely, on Coote degenerate. That Miss Oates sometimes took football, as he did himself, for the sake of the children, was unfeminine and foolish; that Coote wouldn't, not even for the sake of the children, was unmanly and perverse. No phrase of Coote's, no movement, did not jar. His nasal cockney grated. The dull sheen of his lank, blond, curly locks, the flightiness of his hands, the smell of his after-shave, disgusted him. The adages he tossed—'The worst children make the best coppers!', 'Use rough paper! It saves correcting!'—affected Mr Bluett's breathing like poisonous grenades. That such a twank be permitted to work as his superior in a school endowed by public money contributed to his addiction to the bottle. The views on Nigel of a guttersnipe posturing as a progressive teacher would be twenty times more spurious than what had gone before. The views of Lady Sandra and Miss Oates were misguided, often ingenuous. The views of Coote would be tainted by an insalubrious brew of gall and mischief acquired, Mr Bluett was sure of it, from questionable contacts during leisure hours.

'Lacks seriousness and stability.'

Word for word what I'd have written about you!

'Requires constant supervision.'

And why not? With your 'indirect teaching', 'Let the child find out for himself', 'Activity and experience in place of passive assimilation of the facts', you hide your inadequacy of leadership behind American theory. Nigel needed taking by the hand. To ignore him was criminally negligent. If he had reached an average level of competence in the basic subjects, then and then only would you have been justified in leaving him sometimes to his own devices.

Particular Abilities and Interests: 'None.'

You mean he wouldn't blow into a bottle, and thus take part in your atonal, arhythmical musical improvisations; he couldn't extemporise at your behest in drama; he preferred the representational to the abstract. Did it ever occur to you that such a boy might need the security of a fixed number of beats to the bar; that he might be too ashamed of his diction to speak on a stage aloud; that, in Art, your open-ended choices of Polyfilla, crêpe, vitreous stones and pipe-cleaners bewildered him?

Special needs: 'A gag.'

Highly comical! What about his fatherlessness? What about his sexual precocity? What, to put it crudely, about his colour? Doesn't every coloured boy have special needs? If so, in Nigel's case, neither you nor your collaborators have faced them squarely.

'Only reads Football Annuals.'

So you stood by! You left a lost child meandering!

Oral expression: 'Dumb when speech is required of him. A virtuoso of uncalled-for comment.'

Written Expression: 'Output minimal.'

Maths: 'Cannot perceive relationships.'

Mr Bluett mopped his brow.

He broached the subject angrily next morning.

'I've read the record sheets! I know what each one of you said about Nigel!'

'They're not Top Secret, are they?' Colin Coote gulped at his coffee, then, plonking his mug down on the floor, spilled some on the carpet. 'Whoops!'

'I don't consider you've been fair! Any of you!'

'Fair?' This was from Lizzie Oates. '*You* use the word "fair"! You who bait the unfortunate boy at every opportunity! I'm beginning to think the relationship is rather off-colour!'

'Withdraw that remark!'

Lady Sandra endeavoured to dampen the flames:

'If I wrote anything too beastly, I'm prepared to amend it.'

'It must be the spring!' smirked Colin Coote. 'The rising of the sap's exhausting all of us. I suppose the naughty bullfinches are already eating your japonica buds, Lady Sandra!'

Coote and Oates swayed and spluttered on their chairs. Stony-faced, Lady Sandra continued stitching.

Mr Bluett stumped from the room.

On the way to the sanctuary of the Men's, he met the Fuehrer.

'Who's been tampering with the geyser? The pilot flame's gone out again!'

'I suggest you speak to our young Deputy.'

'I have.'

'Perhaps it was the draught.'

'Another matter. My cleaner has been finding fault again.'

'Tell Miss Hodge.'

'It's a man to man concern.'

'Oh very well! But my children await me. Don't make a meal of it!'

'She's a fair and patient woman, so I don't think she's exaggerating when she says she is having to deviate from her authorized weekly quota of 8.8 minutes for the Gentlemen's Toilet.'

'Are you imputing, sir, that I waylay her?'

'I am imputing that her Toilet Work Specification is to wash the hand-basin with a damp cloth and scouring powder, to dust the window-sill and fittings with a damp duster, and to sweep the floor and lino-mat with an impregnated mop—all in under two minutes. This time requirement it has frequently been impossible for her to fulfil due to unhygienic spillages.'

'In other words, Mr Coote can't aim straight.'

'My cleaner complains not of Number Ones but of dollops on the seat.'

'I can assure you I wouldn't deign to sit on the same bus let alone the same thunderbox as that ruddy little sod!'

The Fuehrer nearly smiled. You rarely got a chance to use such language with a woman at the top. 'Sods are usually so tidy!'

'Musicians aren't supposed to thump. This one's the exception. Now, if you'll excuse me, the desk lids will soon be banging.'

The Men's was where Mr Bluett liked to get away to think and drink and recuperate after rowing with his colleagues.

He took a snifter, then looked at himself in the glass.

Gaunt. Bloodshot. Silver-haired. Weak, watery eyes. The face that had never vanquished Muriel. The face that would never vanquish Nigel? Should he scuttle? Was his chosen task too onerous? Wasn't he aboard a shell, a galleon without sails, a drifting hulk whose weak she-skipper surrendered in turn to the impulsiveness of the weather and all hands?

134

He laughed. A former soldier, he was quite at sea! 'This should be rum not brandy! Easy now! Flask away! Wash paws. Steady. Open sesame. Nigel, here I come!'

He staggered through the door towards his classroom. He laughed again. What good were Latin, cricket, the Queen's English and conventional mathematics to a Nigel?! And wasn't it too late for this Mess-spoilt failure to visit the Black Continent and pick up trumpet playing, voodoo and under-water harpooning at first hand? The trouble with drink was it raised as many doubts as those it stilled!

The behaviour of the children was strangely muted when he reached them. Mr Coote had called for Miss Hodge.

'The racket coming from Mr Bluett's room . . . I've been in three times. What do you suggest?'

'Where is Mr Bluett?'

'He left the staff-room five minutes before the bell. The toilet door is locked. He may be ill.'

This would stir her. She had a soft spot for Bluett.

'He'll be indulging his little weakness. Can't you call him out, Mr. Coote? I don't want to appear to be prying. There was a nasty incident last term involving Lorraine's parents. I want him to recover his morale.'

Coote lost his temper.

'Mr *Bluett*'s morale! What about mine?! I go three times to his classroom. Three times I call for order. Three times the noise grows louder than before. The reason I get no response is well-known. It's due to your . . .'

'Due to my what, Colin?'

'To your . . . unhelpfulness! How can we survive term after term against the children without your support?'

He was almost in tears.

'Deary me! I never guessed you thought me so inaccessible!'

She went upstairs and punched some backs and walloped several legs.

'So quiet!' said Mr Bluett. 'So unearthly quiet! Has there been an accident?' The walls and floor were dithering. 'Has someone been hurt?' He wiggled his fingers at them in a funny way. They'd never seen him as drunk as this before.

'You can say *that* again, sir! Miss 'Odge thumped Gary!'

135

'And me, sir! Mr Coote got 'er. She's called the Register and taken Dinner Money.'

'Mr *Coote* got her? I'll wring his neck! Go to Assembly! Get out of my sight, the lot of you! No! Nigel wait behind!'

Christ! This was too early to be tipsy.

'Nigel, run to the staff-room and make me a cup of coffee! The very best! Nothing but the black! . . . Half a moment! I'm not asking you to do it because I hate you. I want you to understand that. I'm asking you because I love you. I want you to trust me, Nigel. Above all else I want you to trust me. I wonder if you take my meaning. Now, if I tell you a secret, will it forge a bond between us? . . . I am asking you a question. If I tell you a secret, will it forge a bond between us?'

Nigel was frightened. Mr Bluett was gripping him by the shoulders.

'Take sugar, sir?'

'Take sugar, sir! Take sugar! Of course I take sugar, you cheeky, you adorable . . . Do you know what you are? You're an agent provocateur . . .'

Nigel tried to move.

'But I haven't told you my secret yet!'

'You're drunk, sir!'

'Oh, that's no secret! My secret is this: I despise Mr Coote. I want you to gain something from that piece of information, son. You don't mind my calling you "son", Nigel? Because, believe it or not, I consider you my son! Nigel, I want you to mark, learn and inwardly digest that I despise Mr Coote! Despise him! And Mr Coote's a white man! Understand? I despise him, and he's not a nigger, not a wog, not a coon, not a spade—he's a sneaky invertebrate out-and-out white rotter, and I expect you to despise him too!'

'I don't want to despise him, sir!'

'But he used to confiscate your football! I've never done that, have I? I've even put you on the football team!'

'Yes, but . . .'

'But what?'

Coote's pounded rendering of 'Daisies are our silver, Buttercups our gold' wafted upwards from the hall.

'I just liked him, sir.'

'You're sure of that, are you? Quite, quite sure? He didn't

like you, you know! He didn't like you one little bit! He wrote all sorts of untrue things about you on your record. So did Miss Oates. So did Lady Sandra . . .'

Nigel wriggled free, and fled. The coffee never came.

Mr Bluett began to pave the way for cricketing next term: 'Good news, eh, that England's regained the Ashes?'

Nigel pulled a 'So what?' face.

'Cassius Clay lost the fight last night, sir! Frazier won! Whaam! A left hook on the chin—'

Even inter-school football matches on the gravel pitches of Finsbury Park were preferable to boxing.

'Football team or choir?' sneered an African bus conductress on one occasion as the team shouted club-jingles to the tunes of 'Rule Britannia' and 'Land of Hope and Glory'.

'Neither,' blustered Mr Bluett, 'but in this young brother of yours, lie the makings of a bowler and a batsman.'

Nigel pouted. He didn't want to be singled out for special notice. If Brandyguts liked him as he claimed, why wouldn't he allow him to play with stray dogs and watch the passing trains at half-time with the others? Why did *he* have to pass round lemons and then go all over the pitch collecting spat-out rinds?

In English it was the same.

' "Once upon a most early time was a Neolithic man. He was not a Jute or an Angle, or even a Dravidian, which he might well have been, Best Beloved, but never mind why. He was a Primitive, and he lived Cavily in a Cave, and he wore very few clothes, and he couldn't read and he couldn't write and he didn't want to . . ." '

Nigel squirmed.

' "He did not know his own strength in the least. In the Jungle he knew he was weak compared with the beasts, but in the village people said that he was strong as a bull . . ." '

Gary stared at Nigel in wide-eyed admiration. Lorraine tittered nervously. But only when Mowgli shouted, 'They have cast me out from the Man-Pack, Mother!'; only when 'Man-Pack and Wolf-Pack have cast me out,' said Mowgli. 'Now I will hunt alone in the Jungle,' did Nigel consider the story in any way relevant to himself.

' " 'Ahae! My heart is heavy with the things I do not understand,' sang Mowgli as he danced on the hide of Shere Khan, the tiger," '—here, also, Nigel dimly appreciated the truth of Kipling's writing, but none of Mr Bluett's good intentions.

Mr Bluett pledged the future, and wrote of Nigel an over-complimentary profile.

Miss Hodge would not let it pass.

'Listen to this! "Given time, Nigel's written work, imaginative and factual, may well usurp his undoubted flair as a con-versationalist and as a sportsman."!!'

'The iron at last is hot. The forging will be easy.'

'Hmm.'

'You doubt me?'

'I doubt Nigel. We can't give this particular boy an advantage merely because he's black.'

'Nigel *needs* a grammar school, not a ghetto comprehensive! Some of us are late developers. Intellect isn't a static thing!'

'Sorry, Francis! I'm not convinced.'

'Listen, Muriel! I've at last got Nigel where I want him. He's happy with soccer. He's a good athlete. He'll be as good at cricket. He has a hobby now—collecting stamps. I've begun this year's project on the Commonwealth, something with which he can for once identify. Give me till next term to raise the standard of his English and his Maths!'

'I shall. And you can record your findings in his Supplementary Report. Meanwhile I'm destroying this, and will write the truth as *I* see it.'

She tore his handiwork in pieces, and delivered them to the basket.

'Don't look so downcast! Nigel will find his level eventually, whichever one of us is right.'

He remained sitting in front of her, fumbling with the turn-ups of his trousers.

'That will be all, Francis. But take my advice! Distance your-self from the boy. You are overloading him.'

'Implying I am harming him?'

'Nigel, more like, is harming you!'

The Fuehrer strutted in, without announcement, carrying a broken lampshade.

'Nigel again!'

'Don't blame Nigel!' smiled Miss Hodge. 'Nigel, according to Mr Bluett, can do no wrong. Isn't that so, Mr Bluett?'

'If that's the case, Madam, I leave the matter in *your* capable hands!' He placed the remnants of the shade on the blotting pad before her. 'And may I also, Madam, draw your attention to the fact that the gas jets in the hall are being extinguished daily. The same scoundrel, I shouldn't won—'

'Oh, another time! Another time!'

He blinked at her and scratched his head.

'Madam! There could be an explosion!'

'Whereupon our troubles would be at an end!'

At the Schools' Reception Desk of the Commonwealth Institute, Mr Bluett collected a sheaf of questionnaires about West Africa, then climbed to the first floor to distribute them.

'Look at the chief's court in Ghana. What is the little boy holding?'

The boy was holding an umbrella. Nigel wrote it was a television aerial.

'Find three foods eaten by people who live in West Africa.'

Nigel, instead of plaintains, maize, yams or sweet potatoes, put grasshoppers, Yorkshire pudding and priests' legs.

'Name three kinds of work done by people in West Africa.'

Mr Bluett had told him that the first cocoa beans were brought from Ghana to Fernando Po in 1879, that Ghana now produced about one-third of the world's supply. He had shown him the diorama of fishing vessels in Takoradi Harbour, also the list of timber exports: wawa, sapele, mahogany, kokrodua and utile. Nigel answered that niggers did no work—they lazed and loved all day among the ashanti blood plants of the jungle.

Nigel wanted to forget his origins. These exhibits humiliated him. He considered that he was being laughed at—worse, that he was being pitied.

When Brandyguts asked him to come and inspect some Ghanaian postage stamps, he rebelled. He ran away to the grown-ups canteen and stole a doughnut. Then he dashed out of the building and threw stones at ducks and trod on wallflowers.

An attendant with a gammy leg returned him in a vice-like grip to the distraught Mr Bluett who was scanning for him in the vestibule.

'This yours?'

Nigel was rubbing his arm and whingeing.

'Indeed yes! Thank you so much!'

'Rather you than me!'

'Oh, I don't know! Boys will be boys!'

'Call that a boy?! Animal more like! Destroying the flowers outside, he was! And trying to kill the ducks!'

Mr Bluett, from the extreme of demanding from Nigel nothing but the best, forgave him.

'No need to be insulting!'

'Insulting! I haven't started yet! I'd lock him in a cage if I were you, and chain him to a ring!'

'If I may say so, I find your attitude repugnant.'

'Too bad. Teachers must control their children. I shall be asking for your name.'

'My name is Bluett. Francis Bluett of Adelaide Bing Primary School, Junior Mixed.'

'Mixed is right. You'll be sent a bill for damage, and barred from future admission.'

Mr Bluett surveyed the man's regulation uniform disdainfully. The dormant army officer inside him began to wake. He wanted to bawl, 'Stand to attention!'

'Aren't you rather forgetting your rank?'

'I'd forget anything if it'd prevent the entry into this country of nignogs the likes of him!'

He jerked a thumb at Nigel.

'Does the ideal of Commonwealth mean nothing to you, then?'

'There are nignogs and nignogs, aren't there?'

'White honky!' Nigel yelped.

'Watch it, son! Watch it!' threatened the attendant with an upheld fist.

'All right! I'll deal with him!' intervened Mr Bluett.

'I hope you do—and hard!' growled the attendant, limping off.

'Why, why, why, Nigel? What gets into you? You change so swiftly!'

Nigel tugged away from the blue-veined hands which held him.

'Behave like someone I can be proud of, Nigel—not like the

140

rest of the riff-raff in my charge! Look at them brawling there!
Listen to their hullabaloo! Rude. Inconsiderate of others. Please,
please don't be like one of *them*! Come on! Don't glower! Wipe
away those tears. Here! Take my hanky! Better? Good! Now
then, want me to buy you something to prove there's no hard
feelings, that bygones are bygones? You know, I'm *not* the heart-
less old disciplinarian you seem to take me for! We can all lose
our tempers. I have forgotten already how you've behaved this
afternoon. How would you like this poster here on African
stamps?'

Half an hour ago Nigel had run away to escape Africa, and
African stamps in particular. This, then, was Brandyguts' cun-
ning way of punishing him, of rubbing his nose in it, of making
him swallow the same medicine twice while pretending to be a
good guy!

'It'll do!'

'Well sound a bit more enthusiastic! "I'd like it *very much*"!'

'I'd like it *very much*!'

' "I'd like it very much *indeed, thank you*"!'

'I'd like it very much, *indeed, thank you*!'

' "I'd like it very much indeed, thank you *sir*"!'

'I'd like it very much indeed, thank you, *sir*!'

'*That's* better!'

'*That's* better!'

'Oh dear! When *are* we going to lose our chip?'

To be teacher's pet was one degree worse than being teacher's
enemy. For the rest of term, Nigel was as insulting as he knew
how.

'Nigel! What happened to the daffodil bulb Lady Sandra
gave you?' Mr Bluett asked before the arrival of the judge from
the Flower Lovers' League.

'I gave it to Lorraine.'

'He did not, sir!'

'Yes I did!'

'Liar! Black Pudding!'

'That will be enough, Lorraine! Nigel, you'll have to do better
than that!'

'The cat ate it.'

'So the cat ate it, did he?'

'It's a she.'

'You haven't a cat at all, have you?'

'No.'

'How did a cat eat your bulb, then?'

'It belongs to the man next door!'

His teeth flashed bright at this success.

Mr Bluett took to drinking in the classroom from an opaque plastic bottle.

'My gourd. My gourd of water!' The children buzzed with disbelief. Lorraine peeped at Nigel through a fence of fingers. 'I recommend the beverage to each of you, now the days are lengthening. Lent, lengthen, warmer, must have water. Cause and effect. Everything has its reason, if we only bother to find out!'

There was gossip on the Magnolia Estate:

'Poor luv! They say he tipples during lessons!'

On the way to the last League match of the season, Nigel trampled through shrubberies and banged his boots against car mudguards.

'Up and coming Borstal?'

'You've got a right one there!'

'Don't envy you *him*, mate!'

'Teachers bloody well deserve every holiday they get!' . . .

Mr Bluett resented the public's condolences. They confirmed his failure.

'Nigel!' he shouted. 'Where's your self-respect?!'

Nigel indulged in a mock search through all his pockets.

'Pull yourself together!'

Nigel pretended to tie his limbs into a neat parcel.

He ran to Mr Bluett at half-time. Adelaide Bing were losing.

'Sir! Sir! Their centre forward called me "Nigger" and attacked me with a knife!'

'Who?!'

'Him, sir!'

'Come to me, that boy!'

Everyone gathered round.

'Fish and Chips here called me "Nigger"!' Nigel explained.

'Didn't!'

'Did!'

'Didn't!'

142

'Come on! Give it to me!'

Mr Bluett stretched a hand out for the knife.

'Give you what, sir?'

'You know what! Come on! Don't look so innocent! I want that knife!'

'*Knife*?!!'

There was no knife. Mr Bluett had to apologize profusely.

'Nigel! Hand round the lemons! That was very silly!'

'I'll get you afterwards, old Brandyguts, you pickled gherkin!'

Only Hennessy and a chance diatribe in an Earl's Court shop, where he was buying some sugar, held Mr Bluett to his purpose.

'Don't bother to wrap it up!' he said.

'Not like the darkies we get in here!' bantered the assistant. 'The first words they must learn when they come over here are "Put it in a bag! Put it in a bag!". It doesn't matter what it is—a tin of beans, an orange, a bar of chocolate, a packet of cigarettes—"Put it in a bag! Put it in a bag!!" Peculiar! Put the whole ponging lot of *them* in a bag *I* would, and post them back to where they belong! Who the hell do they think they are, anyway, telling *us* what to do?!'

'Remember, Roman, thy high destiny!' retorted Mr Bluett and strode imperiously into the street without his sugar.

'A fine game! A grand game!' Mr Bluett soliloquized, as Nigel helped him count stumps and bails and sort pads and gloves at the start of the summer term. 'The best thing in cricket is to win; the next to lose; the worst not to play!' Nigel didn't look convinced. 'Yes, and you'll be our best bowler! We'll soon groove that swing of yours. How tall are you? Good. The taller the better.'

The only thing that mattered at the moment to Nigel, and to every other child at Adelaide Bing, was football—namely, England's First Division Soccer Championship. Arsenal, the neighbourhood team, was due to meet Spurs in the League Final at White Hart Lane. At nets, to which Lorraine and a few other girls were admitted due to paucity of volunteers, there were cries of 'We want football!', 'We are the Champions!', 'Up the Gunners!' 'We hate Tottenham Hotspur!'

It was not so much Nigel's aversion to nets that prompted a visit by his teacher to his home, as his offering for sale, at the School Bring and Buy, the Cricketers' Almanack Mr Bluett had so kindly lent him.

Magnolia Court was one of several tall, grey tenements spaced around an arid lawn. The 'development' would have resembled a futurist repair station for automata save that, tonight, there were accessories—red and white scarves and rosettes, cardboard footballs and photographs of Arsenal players—hung in every lighted window, and looped streamers linked flower-box to flower-box, household to household, in a common human bondage.

The stinking lift, a coffin lined with fluted steel, scraped to the eighth storey where shielded lights jutted at regular intervals from metal brackets in a lengthy corridor. Mr Bluett's footsteps clacked between the naked concrete floor and a low grey shiny ceiling. The wall-tiles were sky-blue. The primrose doors, symmetrically spaced, were identical but for their numbers.

He pressed the two-note bell of No 84.

They'd be watching Friday's cowboy series. He wouldn't criticize Nigel. He'd ask for explanations. He would tread warily, win the mother's trust, not bludgeon her into defiance.

A fleeting shadow cast across frosted panes materialized.

'Yes?'

'I'm Nigel's teacher.'

'Mr Bluett? Come inside. Let me take your hat. Nothing wrong, I hope?'

She was polite for Nigel's sake. This bullying oddity could influence her son's future.

She ushered him into a 'lounge' where nothing matched, where a tiger-striped carpet and thrush-egg wallpaper and kingfisher upholstery and salmon curtains competed to aggravate the eye. A woollen owl, perched on a gilded mirror, had pride of place over a nacre-encrusted fishing smack, a china nanny-goat and a large felt bull, encumbered with banderillas and an Arsenal rosette. A budgie fidgeted behind bars. Nigel, cross-legged, gazed at television in a corner.

'Turn that off, Nigel! Look who's here!'

Nigel started. Did his enemy intend to invade his home life now as well?

'Be a good boy. Pour both of us a drink. Mr Bluett, what will you have? Sherry or lager? There's brandy if you prefer it.'

She said the last casually.

'Brandy, please. Only a dash of water.'

'Sherry for me, dear. Want a coke for yourself?'

'No, thanks, Mum.'

So surprising was it to see Nigel play Prince Charming, Mr Bluett neglected to introduce the purpose of his visit. Glasses were raised, pleasantries exchanged.

'And where, Mr Bluett, are you off to this year for your well-earned summer holidays?'

She wanted a good secondary school for Nigel. Hence her continued deference.

'I've made no plans. And the two of you?'

'Cala Mesquida. Pontin's did us proud again last year. I

suppose you've noticed some of our souvenirs—the boat there, that bull. You bought them as presents for me, didn't you, Nigel? He's wonderfully kind to his Mum, Mr Bluett, is Nigel.'

That should impress.

Mr Bluett wasn't sure where Cala Mesquida was.

'You know Majorca?'

Saved! 'By repute, of course.'

He must try to get away more often, instead of just drifting between Earl's Court and Lord's.

'Nigel! You never told me!'

'You never asked.'

'Have you ever seen a bullfight?'

'Certainly not!' the mother interjected. 'I let him buy me the bull, though. Admire its rosette? Who do you think will win the match on Monday week?'

Mr Bluett didn't care.

'Arsenal, I imagine.'

'Let's drink to that! The Gunners!'

Why do so many coloured people seize on the basest pleasures our society has to offer? thought Mr Bluett. He was tempted to mention his cricketing plans for Nigel, but the moment seemed inappropriate. He retraced the path of conversation.

'What do you remember best about your Majorca holiday, Nigel?'

'Vichy water.'

'*Vichy* water?'

'Yes!' Mum stared at son approvingly. 'We rarely risked the common Spanish variety.'

Mr Bluett was stumped for an adequate rejoinder. He felt old and out of touch. 'Anything else?'

'We sank in the sand, didn't we, Mum? And we saw a field-mouse when we were walking through a forest. And there was a drummer drumming in the hotel band and two people were on the floor dancing—one was a life-saver and he was sweating as if a bucket of water had been thrown over him.'

'That's not all, Nigel. What did we notice about the schools?'

'They looked like huts?'

'And the carts the donkeys pulled?'

'They were painted red and yellow so car headlights could pick them out at night.'

What was the secret of this power the woman possessed over her son? In what was he, his teacher, so deficient as to make this difference between Nigel's manner at school and here at home? Of the boy's basic loveliness he was now convinced. Yet what set him at odds with the one of them and not the other?

'Nigel, it's your bedtime. Pour Mr Bluett another drink, then off with you. We grown-ups have things we want to talk about.'

Working in Tesco's! Hair wrapped in a chiffon bandanna like in every cartoon caricature. Yet she showed the tact of a diplomat, the intuition of a nun! He needed the drink that Nigel handed him.

'Now say goodnight to Mr Bluett! I'll tuck you up in half an hour. Make sure the bath water isn't too hot! Have you a book to read?'

He nodded.

It couldn't be true! They were conspiring! 'Have you got a book to read?'! 'Make sure the bath water isn't too hot!'! Nigel came to school as bleary from watching late night movies, and as smelly, as the rest.

'Go on! Say goodnight to Mr Bluett!'

'Goodnight, sir.'

'Goodnight, Nigel. See you on Monday. No smoking meantime! We've a cricket practice, remember?' He laughed heartily.

'Well now. Why are you here?'

She whisked a cover over the budgie's cage as though to spare it the ugliness of what might ensue. Her voice had a harder ring. She resented, for a start, Mr Bluett's joke about smoking.

'Nigel's a very fine young fellow, but he's causing me a lot of worry.'

'His other teachers seemed satisfied enough! . . . I do my side as best I can. You know, of course, there isn't no father?'

This was the first time since arriving that he had heard her grammar slip.

'You appear to be managing admirably. It is *I* who have failed. I seek advice.'

'I can't advise you how to teach any more than you can advise me how to be a mother.'

'His behaviour at school has been appalling.'

'Maybe there's nothing there to interest him.'

'But even during football he runs wild!'

'You've seen him here tonight. If you're suggesting I can't control him—'

'Not at all!'

'Good. We parents are sick and tired of being told by schoolmasters and schoolmarms how to bring up our children!'

'Quite, quite! It's just that every day for Nigel at the moment seems to be an April Fools' Day. Worse. I found on sale at the Bring and Buy the copy of Wisden I lent him.'

'Wisden?'

'The Cricketers' Almanack.'

'I'm sorry. I assure you, if I'd known . . .'

'I suppose I must have unconsciously provoked the insult.'

She hedged. She knew that Nigel hated Bluett and thought that he unduly picked on him.

'You've never ridiculed the Gunners?'

'I've substituted cricket for football. But it's the season.'

'I'll call him if you wish.'

'No! But why my Wisden of all things? He's a promising cricketer. I want him for the school side.'

'Perhaps he finds the game is rather slow.'

'It will help me write a good supplementary report. For his next headmaster, you understand.'

'I see. I'll have a word with him. He tells me nothing about school no more.' Another slip. 'He used to tell me plenty. He asked for odds and ends for making things. Mr Coote had a class orchestra.'

'He still does.'

'Nigel made a double-bass. I brought him a crate and a length of timber all the way from Tesco's. Never a dull moment! He worshipped the ground Mr Coote walked on. Miss Oates, too. What a lively girl! All those experiments of hers! He practised them here and in the kitchen. Stacking books and comics on an egg-shell. It carried thirty pounds! Then he boiled water in a paper cup over a candle flame. And, did you know, if you draw black squares in rows on a white background . . .?'

'Yes, yes! Miss Oates can be very stimulating!'

'And Lady Sandra, bless her heart! Nigel makes fun of her, but he listens to what she says. How's her garden, by the way? How I laughed when her marmalade cat, Pussy Pringle, went

148

deaf and couldn't hold sensible conversations! Nigel was only seven then, and loved it!'

'And now, I suppose, he resents the hard grind and learning what will be of use to him at his next school, wherever that may prove to be?'

'I agree there comes a time when we have to sober up.'

'Sober up'. She watched to see if the ill-considered phrase had caused offence. Indeed, she held an armoury of reported gossip as ammunition in case of any confrontation. With her son's next school, though, still at stake, she decided it was untimely to attack.

'I don't want him mollycoddled, Mr Bluett. Boys, especially boys without a father, need a firm hand where it hurts but doesn't harm.'

'A brave remark, but Miss Hodge wouldn't openly agree with you, and I refuse to continue being Adelaide Bing's behind-the-scenes disciplinarian, an unpaid mercenary, as it were, for all that's officially disallowed.'

'If a child tried to sell my property—my "Wisden" did you call it?—I'd lay him across my knee and thrash him!'

'I thought that, to show there was no ill-feeling on my part, I might diminish his resentment by some act of kindness. A week-end outing, perhaps? A Saturday at Lord's?'

'It's as you please, Mr Bluett.'

She'd have demurred were it not for the impending 'report'. To conceal her agitation, she crossed to the window and drew the curtains.

The doorbell rang.

'Thank you for calling!' She hustled Mr Bluett into the hall. 'Give me warning next time. If there *is* a next time, which I sincerely hope there won't be. You got your Wisden back, I hope?'

'Never mind. All takings go to swell our School Fund.'

'Thank you, Mr Bluett! Don't forget your hat! I suppose you'll be going to the great football match?'

'No!'

'Oh . . . Now, remember what I said, don't let Nigel get the better of you! He'll have to behave himself on School Journey when it comes to June, won't he? It *is* you who's going with Miss Hodge as usual, isn't it?'

'Yes, indeed!'

'What a pity!' she thought.

She opened the door. Standing on the threshold was an impatient negro, with a bunch of red and white roses in his fist and an Arsenal scarf draped round his shoulders.

'It's OK, Harry,! This is only Mr Bluett, Nigel's teacher. Goodbye, Mr Bluett! Come in, Harry! Don't stand about!'

'Up the Gunners!'

Harry roughly pushed the roses towards her and banged the door behind him.

Whoever Harry was, Mr Bluett disliked him.

The neighbourhood bubbled like a cauldron. All roads to White Hart Lane were paved with belligerent intentions. North London was a bedlam. Bottles were thrown. Beware the man who supported Spurs!

Adelaide Bing became a betting shop. It wasn't *who* would win, but Arsenal by how much. Pictures of star players changed hands for chewing-gum and crisps. Lorraine and other girls were physically aroused. Mr Bluett was alarmed. Should he consult Lizzie Oates? What if their muliebrity were made premature? What if there were faintness, nausea and bloodstains? The whole shocking business was too vile to contemplate.

He wrote to Nigel's mother :

'Thank you for receiving me so graciously. I understand the awkwardness of unexpected calls.' This was a veiled reference to the rose-bearing Harry. 'I am very conscious of having failed Nigel.' Insincere. Hadn't Nigel failed *him*? 'It is obvious that my classroom methods are not as entertaining as those of my colleagues. The fact remains—and we touched on this—I have to consider the requirements of his next school. What about having him as *Captain* of the cricket team?' That should sway her! 'Have you any objection to my taking him on Saturday the 25th to watch the MCC play Pakistan at Lord's? I remember you agreed to the idea of such an outing. I just hoped you had not yourself made other plans for him on that particular date. Thanking you in anticipation. Let's hope some, if not all, behaviour problems will be resolved thereby! . . .'

He posted the letter. He had misgivings. Was it obvious that Nigel had become an idée fixe?

150

Nigel's mother had misgivings too, but she believed she needed Mr Bluett's helpful reference. She reasoned, therefore, that Nigel must learn to tolerate all sorts—white people, peculiar people, yes, even dangerous people. He must fend for himself. His instincts would protect him.

It took her some days to formulate a reply. Tesco's did not employ her in the stockroom for her spelling, and Harry's spelling was no better than her own. She borrowed a dictionary from the manager.

Mr Bluett meanwhile drank too much. He hadn't felt so nervous since awaiting exam results at Sandhurst.

'You might have given me time to prepare!' he snapped at Coote who called on him from the piano one morning to take Assembly during Muriel's absence at the dentist.

'How was I to know she'd be away!' retaliated Coote. 'She tells me nothing.'

'No need for disloyalty. You're her paid henchman, aren't you?'

'Oh *I'll* do it!'

'No you won't!'

'Make up your mind!'

Even allowing for the euphoria, even allowing for the fact that Arsenal won the Soccer Championship the night before and North Londoners had danced the conga through the lamplit streets, Mr Bluett's abilities as a disciplinarian showed patent signs of deterioration.

'There's a correct way of sitting. Backs straight. No lounging. Look at me. Now, without a sound, Hymn No 139—"Onward Christian Soldiers". Silence! Very well! Hands on head. No, put your books on the floor first. Hands down. We'll try again. Hymn No 139. Stand without talking. I said, "*without* talking". Gary! Nigel! Sit everyone. Silence. That's better. Stand. Sit. Stand. Hymn books in both hands. Ready? After four . . .'

By the second chorus, 'Onward Christian Soldiers' had become 'Onward good old Arsenal marching to the Cup'. Mr Bluett stopped Coote at the piano again and again.

'Now eyes closed and hands together for the Lord's Prayer. *Without* dropping your hymn books. No, don't put them on the floor. Tuck them under your left arm. "Our Father . . ." Stop!

Who said "Our Ray Kennedy"? Nigel? I'm surprised at you. Tell us. Who *is* Ray Kennedy?'

Hubbub.

'Do you think God is interested that Ray Kennedy is Arsenal's skipper?'

'Yes, and I bet he hopes he'll win the Cup Final on Saturday!'

Cheering.

For his address after the Lord's Prayer, Mr Bluett extemporized that the better team, be it Arsenal or Liverpool, would win the FA Cup; he doubted whether God knew there was a Cup Final but, if He did, he was positive He didn't care. Several children booed. Provoked, he made everyone bow their heads and pray that the better side, the English or the Pakistani, would win the Tests.

Nigel, for raising the matter of Ray Kennedy, had to bear the brunt of his displeasure in the classroom afterwards.

'Why are you late?' 'Doing up my shoe-lace.' 'Rubbish!'

'Why are you on the wrong page?' 'I'm not on the wrong page!' 'Poppycock!—Stop sniggering, Lorraine!' 'I'm not sniggering!' 'Niggering, then!'

Nigel's mother hastened to her writing pad.

'Sorry for the delay. Don't blame Nigel. I am very pushed at work. Delighted you think Nigel's good enough to be Captain of the cricket team. I am very happy about him going to Lord's. I'll put a tablet in his pocket in case he gets the runs . . .'

Jubilation! Sympathetic Dame of Nature! He forgave her 'Mr' on the envelope. He excused her awkward spelling of 'sincerely'. How charming was 'runs' as an unintended pun! It was not surprising such a woman had a beau! Arsenal for the double! Let everyone rave and shout and change their scarves, rosettes, streamers, stickers and dangling dolls from red and white to yellow and blue! Why shouldn't the hoi polloi have their fun! We are the Champions! We hate Liverpool! On to Wembley! Arsenal for the Cup!

He indulged the children in their chatter.

'Dad says they'll have to get the defence on the wrong foot.'

'They'll be all right if they don't use too much steam in the first half.'

'Hope they build up fast and use the space on the flanks!'

'Yes, they're done for if they play too tight!'

Capital! Capital!

Nigel was far from being so tolerant of the idea of himself and Mr Bluett at Lord's.

'Mum! Why must I go?'

'It's for your own good! You'll do everything he tells you to!'

'Won't!'

'You bloody well will!'

'Ratbag!'

She clipped him smartly across the face.

'Let the bugger take you to Lord's! You're to be Captain of that school cricket team and that's an order!'

'Will Uncle Harry take me to the Victory Parade?'

'Yes, if Arsenal win!'

Arsenal did win—2—1 after extra time, so Nigel got his parade and rattled a rattle and carried a banner and saw his football 'immortals' drive through bedizened streets waving silver trophies.

'Why can't life always be magical like this?' he wondered.

'I'm sorry!' Mr Bluett addressed the class. 'We've now got to settle down. Let's forget football for a term, shall we? This is summer, and the first main job on our hands is to get together our cricket team. We're due to play St Bridget's not long after School Journey. Hands up the lunchtime volunteers?'

No hands.

'Well Nigel's volunteered for a start. I have a nice letter saying so from his mother. Jolly good, Nigel! Thanks a lot! Encouraging to have someone who's keen. Anyone else? Girls? Remember you're included! Lorraine? Yes, I thought you would! Gary? Excellent!'

When Gary agreed, others grudgingly followed suit.

'Still two required. Come along! We can't have an Irish-sounding school like St Bridget's beat us at our own game, can we?!'

No one else could be persuaded.

'Very well, then. Nearer the day, perhaps. Not a bad response, though. My thanks to everyone concerned!'

They'd never seen him so compliant, so bright and breezy. He seemed to be as pleased with Arsenal's double win as they were. Someone started 'For he's a jolly good fellow!' Nigel conducted. Gary shouted, 'Three cheers for Brandy Bluett!' at the end.

Mr Bluett was delighted.

'All write out a hundred times "I must not call my betters by their nicknames"!'

Sentimentality thus reverted to resentment. Less than the original nine turned up for playground practices.

Lizzie Oates twitted him:

'I believe there's to be another deathly hush in the close at lunchtime! How's the future Learie Constantine shaping?'

'A treat, Miss Oates. Thank you for inquiring!'

Sarcastic little minx! She's probably been spying! Nigel couldn't hit the ball, and his bowling was erratic.

'Nigel!' he advised next week. 'Perhaps you shouldn't swim. It's putting your eye out.'

'But you told me I *had* to!'

'I've changed my mind. Your ratio of bone and muscle to fat tissue is making you swim too low in the water. It affects your poise.'

'Thanks!' For a quarter of an hour at nets, Nigel tried to concentrate on what Mr Bluett was telling him:

'Watch this—a leg spinner. Quick forward turn of the wrist. *Anti*-clockwise go my fingers, forearm and elbow. If I do it well, the ball is very, very good. Otherwise it's horrid and may cost me the match. Better instead to try an "off". Middle and forefinger at right angles to the seam spread wide and comfortable— thus! Now wedge the ball between them—so! Then spin the ball clockwise with the inner part of the index. Keep Gary on his front foot, make him play forward, and aim on or just outside the off stump. Like that! Right, now you try it!'

Nigel tried it.

'No!!! Aim off! Don't pitch short! Keep the batsman forward! Forward!'

Gary caned the next ball over the wire above the wall and across the road through an upstairs window of a factory.

Touching her lower lip with the tips of her varnished fingernails, Lorraine watched it go.

'What a pretty tinkle!' smiled the Fuehrer coldly, stepping from the outside lavatories trailing a broom and hose.

Lorraine ran her fingers fearfully from lip to burgeoning breasts.

154

One less for nets.

It was always, always the same. Poor initial turn out, and then a falling off, with finally, for the fixture with St Bridget's, a round-up of anybody, whether coached or uncoached, and reliance on a faithful few to win the day.

A complaint came soon, not from the factory but from Miss Walsh. She had stayed behind one lunch hour to type the School Journey programmes and questionnaires. Splinters from a second shattered window, this time her own, had cut her on the forehead.

'I'm not paid danger money, Mr Bluett! You can type them yourself! The key of the duplicator is under the blotter!'

'Miss Walsh! I rely upon you! Won't you re-consider?'

'Not till there's a member of the St John's Ambulance in regular attendance!'

Miss Walsh could be very droll.

Nigel was waiting at the entrance to Magnolia Court, dressed in his best and proudly sporting a camera and a transistor.

'Take them upstairs again! At Lord's you're not allowed use either.'

It wasn't fair! Brandyguts had brought binoculars!

They reached the grounds. Nigel asked could he play on the swings in the graveyard opposite the bus-stop.

'Sorry! We haven't time. Got pencil and rubber for the Score Card?'

'No!'

'As to be expected! You don't bring them to school, so why should you think of them today! It takes two, you know, Nigel, to make an outing a success!'

He bought him a pencil, a rubber, a scoring book and a pictorial history of Lord's and the MCC.

'Would you like "The Laws of Cricket" as well?'

'No!'

'No what?'

'No *thank you*!'

'You see? You can be polite when you try!'

With so much to look at and explain, it was a pity to have to spend precious moments on social training.

'Sure you don't want anything else?' Nigel looked doubtful.

155

He wanted crisps and lemonade. He also wanted a photo of the Pakistani team with their signatures around it. His mother had given him a pound. 'Don't be shy!'

'I'd like that autographed photo!'

'Waste of money. Every signature printed. A total fake.'

Nigel coveted the photo just the same. He would escape and buy it later, and hide it up his jersey.

They sat in the Grand Stand Balcony. Mr Bluett began to lecture :

'Over there, no, to your right, is the Pavilion with its famous Long Room . . .'

Nigel smiled. A man driving a motor-mower looked as though he hadn't a seat under him and was crouched on air.

'And what's so funny about *that*? Oh, by the way, there's the Taverners' special stand . . .'

Batsmen were hitting balls towards the grass incline in front of the Pavilion.

'No! *There*! I do wish you'd concentrate! Not every boy of your sort gets the opportunity of a day at Lord's. Aren't you hot in that jersey?'

Nigel, uncomfortably sticky in the heat, needed somewhere to conceal the photo. Pin-prick perspiration belied his 'No!', so Mr Bluett tried another way.

'These benches can get hard. I don't intend to hire you a cushion when a jersey will do!'

'I want to leave it on!'

'But why?'

'Because.'

'Because what?'

'Just because.'

'Where's your pencil, then? Open your scoring book. Look at the score card. The Pakistanis have won the toss and chosen to bat. Copy out their names. No, first write the date and "MCC v Pakistan" at the top. I'll explain the Bowling Analysis when you've finished. The section for Fall of Wickets you'll find easy. You just write down the full score when each man goes out . . .'

He wished Nigel would remove that damned jersey. It made him thirsty to look at it.

'Written all that? Good. Now I'll explain the Analysis. There are six balls to an over. Right? Six balls, six dots. Whenever a batsman scores, replace a dot by the number of runs. No-balls and wides don't count. They have their own columns on the side. Draw an M through the dots, like so, if no runs are scored during the over . . .'

'Why an M?' wondered Nigel. He didn't dare to ask. Why were the things Brandyguts never mentioned always the most interesting? And why wasn't the girl reading a comic on the seat in front being made to work as hard as he was?

A bell rang. Umpires came out and fixed the bails.

'Applaud the fielders. . . . Now the opening batsmen! Yes, Aftab and Sadiq. Want to look at them through these?' He handed Nigel his binoculars.

A blur. This was misery.

It was misery for Mr Bluett, too. Nigel couldn't, or wouldn't, score properly. He missed the runs; he entered a bye as a leg-bye; he didn't try to recognize the bowlers.

'Oh leave it! We'll watch the scoreboard!'

Should he take a drink from his flask? One end of The Cricketers bar had a space for children. Yet either possibility so early in the game would be setting Nigel a poor example. Brandy, brandy everywhere, and not a drop to drink!

'Sit still, will you!'

'Are you noticing how Ward varies his length and keeps the batsmen on their guard?'

'See how Lever beats the bat almost every time?'

'Sit still!', 'Sit still!', 'Sit still!' . . .

On the way to lunch, Mr Bluett included the Memorial Gallery museum, the squash and tennis courts and the Pavilion in a sweeping gesture:

'Who knows, Nigel! You may belong here some day to enjoy it all! But you won't if you jig on your heels like that!'

The restaurant cashier had a memory for names and faces.

'Good morning, Mr Bluett!'

'Good morning, Mrs Townsend! This is Nigel. Say "Hello, Mrs Townsend"!'

'Hello, Mrs Townsend!'

'Hello, Nigel! What a handsome boy! I have your tickets, Mr Bluett. That'll be one hundred and ninety-four pence, if you please. I believe the batting's rather slow!'

Mr Bluett indicated Nigel.

'Shall we say "solid rather than spectacular"? The tortoise and the hare . . .'

'Well, I'm sure Nigel's having a wonderful time, aren't you, Nigel?'

Before Nigel had a chance to tell the truth, Mr Bluett was recommending use of cloakroom.

'No thanks!'

He didn't want Brandy staring down at him.

'Wait here, then!'

'At the side, dear!' counselled Mrs Townsend. 'There's a queue, I'm afraid!'

There were only tables for four or ten. Mr Bluett chose a 'four' beside the window. A noisy female partnership occupied the better places overlooking the flower-beds.

'Poltergeists!' one was saying. 'I dropped a coffee spoon beside the sofa. Couldn't find it, my dear. *Couldn't* find it! "Don't bother!" I said to myself. "I'll leave it till tomorrow when I'm hoovering." Do you know, I turned that place upside down next morning! Not a sign of it! Had to do the shopping. Came back. Went to put the gas poker in the fire. What should I see staring at me in the face in the middle of the hearthrug? That ruddy spoon!'

'Unexplainable!'

'Inexplic . . .' Mr Bluett restrained himself. Instead, he handed Nigel, bemused by the tale, a copy of the menu.

Nigel's eyes narrowed in panic. But Nigel must learn to fend for himself. After all, it wasn't written in French. Tomato soup, orange juice, roast chicken and vegetable stuffing, braised liver and onions, salmon and salad, gammon ham, ox tongue and salad, new potatoes, garden peas, ice cream, lemon mousse, assorted cheeses, coffee and cream—there was nothing too daunting about that, surely?

'My young companion seems to be having difficulties,' he explained to the waitress. 'Meanwhile, bring me an Armagnac, would you?'

'Yes, sir. Single measure?'

'Double.'

'Soda, sir?'

'Soda and an appreciation of brandy are incompatible.'

The hats of the women bobbed and turned away. He heard

semi-stifled laughter, then a hurried discussion about the creeper on the squash court wall and then the cloudiness of the weather.

Nigel ordered ice-cream, soup and new potatoes.

The women's hats bobbed more-so.

'He'll have orange juice, salmon and salad and strawberry ice-cream. That should cool him down. Nigel, *won't* you remove that jersey! I'll have . . .'

Nigel had gulped away his glass of orange juice before Mr Bluett had taken a first spoonful of tomato soup.

'No need to rush!'

Nigel poured himself some water.

'I'll have some, too. That's better. Always remember others. Mind! You're spilling! Where's your napkin?'

Nigel couldn't cope. He put his salmon in the salad side-dish, poured on vinegar and stirred.

'Well!' exclaimed the waitress. '*He*'s enjoying himself!'

But he wasn't. He was as glad to get away from that restaurant as Mr Bluett.

'At the next meal you eat out, you'll know the ropes a bit better, won't you, Nigel? . . . Say goodbye to the nice waitress!'

'Goodbye nice waitress!'

'Goodbye duckie!'

'Say goodbye to Mrs Towsend!'

'Goodbye Mrs Townsend!'

'Goodbye Nigel!' Aside to another customer—'Isn't it a shame!'

Nigel jumped down four stairs at a time. Outside, he swatted imaginary insects, then ran away as fast as he was able.

Play had recommenced when a drunken Mr Bluett reached his seat. The search for Nigel had given him excuse to tank up at The Full Toss, The Outfield, The Long Stop, The Cricketers and The Father Time. Nigel, who had forestalled him by over half an hour, was beaming blandly.

'Whath there to be tho pleathed about? I've been thcouring the length and breadth of Lord'th for you! And whath that you're holding under your jerthey?'

'Nothing! Leave me alone!'

Mr Bluett raised his binoculars and raked the grounds in search of players.

'Ah, there you all are! Thadiq thtill in? Whath been happening, Nigel? Tell General Brandyguth all about it!'

A shower of rain spared Nigel the pains. Brandyguts stumbled to shelter and strong coffee with Nigel dancing after.

After a more sober return, the commentary began again.

'Notice how rain helps a ball to bounce. The wicket-keeper is taking Ward at shoulder height. The slips are on the alert . . .'

'Did you see Sadiq's turn of the wrist when he hit that four?' . . .

'How's 'at, sir! Out at last! Sadiq caught by Lever at second slip. Why was he caught?'

Nigel didn't know.

'Because he played a crooked bat, that's why! I hope you're gaining from all this. We haven't far to go before St Bridget's.'

Wickets now fell faster.

'Pakistanis don't, of course, meet a lot of rain.'

'Can they grow grass?'

'River water, Nigel. Methods of irrigation taught by Mother England. Let's hope all concerned bear that in mind! The one side of her debt, the other of her obligations!'

After the tea interval—a fizzy drink in The Cricketers for Nigel instead of risking him on thin brown bread and butter elsewhere—and after Pakistan's dismissal for a hundred and ninety runs, England stonewalled over-safely. Nigel couldn't be blamed for being restive. Mr Bluett led him to the Memorial Gallery.

Gripping him above one elbow, he forced him round the exhibits: W. G. Grace's snuff-box, Jack Hobbs' blazer, Don Bradman's boots, a sparrow killed by a ball in 1936 . . .

Nigel's interest flickered. 'Smart!' he whistled.

'Where *did* you learn that hideous expression? Haven't I told you *not* to imitate the worst features of our brethren at Adelaide Bing! "Grand", "terrific", but *never* "smart"! And tell me, what on earth have you got hidden under that confounded jersey?'

As regards School Journey, Miss Hodge was on the horns of a dilemma. Should she recommend that Nigel stay at home, or would to do so smack of racial discrimination? Should she invite the young Colin Coote to take Francis' place, yet didn't she need someone in a balanced state of mind to run Adelaide Bing till her return? Also, with no programmes or questionnaires provided by Miss Walsh this year, wouldn't Colin find a first visit to the Isle of Wight too gruelling?

She asked herself these questions and answered none of them. The staff assumed, and rightly, that she would depart by charabanc for her annual trip in the company of Mr Bluett as was the custom.

Coote could not conceal his disappointment. The experience would have helped with his promotion.

'Why can't *we* go, Liz?' he complained while Mr Bluett was on duty in the playground.

'Hear! Hear! Atten-shun! By the right in two's! Unfortunate kids chivvied year after year from pillar to post by the one of them, while the other does sweet Fanny Adam!'

Lady Sandra, an arachnid in a peasant smock, placed her sewing on her lap. By virtue of not *having* to work, she prided herself on her strict impartiality.

'You must admit you are both rather young!'

Lizzie, in gingham shirt and levis, became bitter and severe. Colin, in a skin-tight suit of peacock green, grimaced coyly:

'What on *earth* has age got to do with it?' he whined.

'Experience!'

'Miss Hodge is superfluous!' objected Lizzie. 'She draws her chalet curtains and lies on her bed.'

'And not alone!' Colin couldn't resist. 'Though this year Brandy will have Nigel, too!'

Lady Sandra stuck to her guns.

'I don't hold any particular brief for Mr Bluett, Colin. But neither am I always impressed by your little sarcasms and impulsive methods . . .'

Oh how Lady Sandra was a bore! She cramped his style!

'Let's face it. He's an alcoholic and a . . .'

Mr Bluett entered the room.

'And then out fell my sewing machine!'—it was Lady Sandra who saw him first.

'What about the billiard cue?'

This was Lizzie's favourite game. You had to keep the conversation rolling without arousing suspicion.

F   161

'Yes, what about the billiard cue?' Colin was determined to stymie Lady Sandra.

'I pushed it up the chimney!'

Mr Bluett was intrigued.

'You had to push a billiard cue up a chimney?'

'My sewing machine fell out. I thought there might be something else up there as well!' She'd never get away with it! Lizzie and Colin were in silent fits. 'My elder boy did it! A prank!'

'Oh, I see!'

Lady Sandra was the winner.

The holiday camp towards which Francis Bluett and Muriel Hodge were destined was set above snow-chalk cliffs, a tawny strand and a turquoise sea. Its open lawns and gardens, its fountain-freshened lake, embodied a town teacher's happiest fancies. Rabbits nibbled safely among saxifrage and vetchling, or scurried in hidden dips sloping to caves and creeks which sounded long ago with chink of pirate treasure. The playful bark of the Manager's dalmatian, the whinny of his pony, the baa of lazy sheep, the drift of distant water through channelled wrack in limpet pools, the blow of cool south-easterlies among willow-herb and madder, the rap of pretty curtains on the alpine frames of quaintly shuttered chalet windows—these and ocean-splendid dawns and sunsets could entreat away the tensions consequent upon school overcrowding and the loneliness of modern slums. So it was here, before the 'season', before the arrival of adults eager to be relieved of thinking for themselves by loudspeakers gaping at the alley angles, that swarms of primary children perennially descended.

Away from the constricting bricks and mortar of Adelaide Bing, Muriel had relaxed already.

A gorse-bush scraped the coach on the Portsmouth Road.

'When *that*, Francis, is out of bloom, love is out of season!'

She continued being 'feminine' when they stopped at Hindhead for refreshments.

'There are more graves dug with a fork than with the bottle!' she quipped as she declined a chocolate éclair.

'Glad to hear you use a fork. It was I who taught you! Incidentally, don't you think that you should stop the children singing? There are soldiers in the café. They deserve a break.'

He did not intend, this year, to spoil her, allow her to back-slide, treat School Journey as a pleasant interlude between doing nothing and doing nothing. Muriel had taken advantage of his chivalry too long. He turned to address a soldier:

'Good life these days in the army?'

'Trained to kill. Want a hand with those caterwauling kids of yours?'

'Is that a criticism?'

'Now that you mention it, yes! Came in here for a bit of hush.'

'Come on children! Out you go!'

They ignored him:

> '. . . Tea for four
> I've got her on the floor . . .'

'Children! That's all! Out!!' Then to the soldier, heartily: 'We started off with "Maybe it's because I'm a Londoner". Football jingles began at Kingston and lasted right through Wisley in to Guildford. Now they've reached the bottom of the barrel. It was "Roll me over in the clover" arriving here! A good old army song eh?! What outfit are you in?'

'RASC—Trainee Division.'

'Passing out soon?'

'Get lost!' . . .

The children screamed into Portsmouth with:

> 'There'll be Brandy, Brandy, terribly drunk and randy
> In the Stores, in the Stores.
> There'll be Brandy, Brandy, terribly drunk and randy
> In the Quartermaster's Stores.'

Muriel Hodge could not fathom why Francis tolerated it. He was losing grip even faster than she'd guessed. She dared not take action, though, and offend his masculinity so soon.

Mr Bluett, on his side, could not fathom Muriel's acceptance of this unprecedented insubordination. Had she failed to grasp that, this year, he had no intention of allowing her to remain withdrawn and disassociated as was her wont? To punish her, he left her to carry her own luggage onto the boat.

'Nigel!' she called. 'Will you help me with this case?'

Nigel was happy to oblige.

Singling out a negro for a menial task! Mr Bluett beckoned someone else.

163

'Nigel! Put that down!'

Muriel registered surprise. Hard was it to believe that, formerly on this ferry, Francis had cosseted her with kindly attentions, placing, often as not, his own coat about her shoulders to protect her from sea-breezes.

The boat shuddered.

'Nigel! Don't stand on the rail! Swimming isn't your forte!'

'Don't pick, pick, pick, Francis! The poor boy's doing no different to the rest!'

Mr Bluett ignored her. He lifted Nigel bodily to a bench on the upper deck, and kept a hold on him.

Nigel swore, Nigel kicked, Nigel eventually slithered free and ran downstairs.

'A recalcitrant? Have you many?'

If only members of the public would keep their well-intentioned curiosity under lock and key!

'Quite a gale!'

Undeterred, the busybody megaphoned his hands:

'Are there many in your party?'

Mr Bluett did not care for the fellow—nor for his blue blazer.

'You might discuss it with my headmistress. She's somewhere aboard. You'll recognize her easily enough. Day-dreaming in a green plastic mack.'

'The name is Wilfred. Wilfred Lacey. Headmaster of Wendale Manor, Rutland. You can tell us by our pink and yellow hats.'

The hats were knitted. Their owners sat beneath them, polite and docile, as if to move might put their souls in jeopardy. Mr Bluett instantly resented everything to do with Wendale Manor. In silence he watched the crew slip moorings from the mainland.

'I might add that this is my twentieth School Journey,' Mr Lacey persisted.

'And my twenty-fifth, since you regard it pertinent to show credentials!'

The Isle of Wight's coastline solidified through the midday mist. Mr Bluett went down a deck to where Nigel and his friends were spitting. Muriel had averted her gaze, and was pretending to study the convolutions of some begging, black-beaked gulls.

'To interfere or not to interfere?' she was thinking. 'How best to aid a man who, until now, has taken the initiatives and, even still, considers himself more capable than I?'

The children ran away at his approach. She crossed to where he stood. She was as disconsolate as he.

'Care for a drink?'

'Do you have to rub it in?! Anyhow, I've had one!'

'Had one? Where?'

'From this well-known flask of mine!'

He waved it in her face. She remained calm, though the gesture was quite uncharacteristic.

'Care for another—in the bar at my expense?'

'A Devil's bribe!'

He turned on his heel before she could turn on hers to hide her anguish.

A man in a blue blazer approached her.

'How do you do! My name is Wilfred Lacey, headmaster of Wendale Manor, Rutland. Your assistant tells me we're equivalents!'

'I'm afraid Adelaide Bing has been blotting its copybook this morning!'

'Little wonder with that bloke you've got to help you! Who or what can he be?'

'Mr Bluett! A law unto himself! I'm Muriel Hodge . . .'

'Destination?'

'Oh, a holiday camp on the south side. The usual arrangement. Cheaper rates before the season.'

'Same here! "Greygates" to be specific.'

'What a coincidence! That's our one, too!'

'Your Mr Bluett—no discipline, it seems, whatever!'

'No, none whatever. None any longer.'

'I'll help where I can. With the heel of my shoe if necessary.'

'Oh, thank you, thank you! But "unofficially", of course!'

At breakfast, next morning, Mr Bluett could not abide her conviviality. Nor could he interpret it. He had left her to her own devices from the moment of arrival. He had failed, even, to pursue his tradition of calling her with a peck on the forehead and a cup of tea. He might not have discovered the whereabouts of her chalet but for its adjacency to his own, and the string between two posts of its verandah supporting her rinsed underwear. Yet Muriel appeared to be accepting his inattentiveness with more than brave determination—with gratitude! It was not her practice to chat at table beyond making the briefest inquiry as to where on such and such a day he might be heading with the children while she rested. At this moment, though, she was prattling with the inconsequence of a teenager at her own party. She was not surprised, she said, that Nigel had left his jersey on the Hyde Pier train. 'Let him find his own way to Newport Depot to collect it, and, if he gets lost or killed, we shall unite in a prayer of thanksgiving!' *That* was the irresponsible mood in which she greeted him today! No interest, beyond a shrug of the shoulders, in the facts that two chalet windows had already been broken and a key thrown in the long grass! No interest in the children now flicking marmalade, and pouring salt in one another's tea! How could she remain glued to her chair, and garrulous and carefree, with Lacey and his tidy-bosomed second in command and all those gutless puppets from Wendale Manor looking on, comparing!

'Have my fried bread, Francis! I want my figure to be right for Prize Day.'

A pat of butter flew from Nigel's direction onto the tablecloth in front of her.

'Whew!' she sighed, patting her hair with one hand and fingering her pierre bleue necklace with the other. 'Isn't it warm today! If you need me, Francis—and I hope you shan't—I'll be catching up on administration in my chalet. Do you leave for Bembridge Windmill immediately after Morning Inspection?'

'I've cancelled Bembridge.'

'But why?'

'We're going to Newport to collect Nigel's lost jersey.'

'A city centre! A jersey! In this heat? Forget it! Everyone can't be penalized because of Nigel!'

'We're going to Newport. The boy has got to learn.'

'And what will he learn?'

'When to leave a jersey on, and when to take it off!'

'Waste! Waste of our coach-price, waste of lovely weather, waste of everything! Francis, you are being pigheaded! I despair of you!'

She toured the chalets with her master key when he had departed. She discovered biscuit crumbs, gum gobs, fouled basins, torpedoed ceilings, smashed window-panes and mirrors, porno-graphic polaroid photos taken by the children of one another. Only Nigel's quarters were in order—pyjamas folded, slippers straight, his mischief obviously set to rights by his protector.

What to do about Francis? How to be kindly in the doing? She put on a pair of sandals, and walked down to the shore to think it all over.

A geologist, poking the rock-face with a stick, was filling a bag with pebbles.

'Splendid spot this for conglomerates!' he said.

She did not dally. She was grieving too much for the days before Francis hit the bottle. He and she were partners then: her promotion to deputy and, later, headmistress, had not yet marred their friendship. Together they had trodden through rich, platonic, chalk-filled days. Curse the quandary of affection versus professional duty! A classroom drinker! She shouldn't have hesitated. The physical and moral welfare of Francis' pupils, of Nigel above all, were in the direst peril. Gratitude for help received had stayed her hand for long enough.

Jumping a rivulet, she hurt her ankle. She hobbled back the way she had come.

Near to the wooden stairs that led to the camp, were Wilfred Lacey's girls and boys, combing the sand for shells and seaweed. One conversed with the geologist. Another was inspecting a fossil with Wilfred's helpmeet. Wilfred was explaining to another: 'No, it's not a sea snail—it's a hermit crab.'

'Good morning, Muriel! Miss Anderson, children! This is Miss Hodge, headmistress of Adelaide Bing, our fellow campers!'

Neither Miss Anderson nor the children seemed pleased to make her acquaintance. 'The dregs!' someone sneered.

Her school 'the dregs!' Keep going, Muriel! Let no one see you weeping!

'Muriel! You're limping!' Wilfred's voice was calling from behind. 'Let me help you! Miss Anderson, you manage on your own, will you?'

A kind voice, a reassuring voice, a voice with authority!

'Forgive me!' He had seen her tears. 'Too, too silly!'

'Lean on my arm!'

She let him guide her. Ironic that Francis used to say, 'You can always lean on me, you know, Muriel. That's what I'm here for!'

'I think I've sprained a tendon.'

'No hurry. Take it easy. When we get back, you can slip off

your stocking and lie on your bed. I'll fetch my First Aid kit and bandage you up. By lunchtime you'll be right as rain.'

She undid her suspenders and rolled off the stocking. With firm hands, Wilfred—or was it Francis?—wrapped away her pain. With firm voice, with untainted breath—no, it was not Francis—he told her to rest quiet.

'Thank you, Wilfred. A culmination of events. I'm better now. Where would I be without your kind consideration!'

'At the mercy of Mr Bluett, God help you!'

'God help *him*! Oh Wilfred, how he worries me! There is no one better intentioned, yet no one capable of doing greater harm!'

'I must go. I hear his coach. For the remainder of your week you can rely on me. When the children are in bed, you'll find me, for the most part, in my chalet. Or may I come to yours?'

'Francis would be jealous.'

She overrated Mr Bluett's dwindling love of her. Nigel's jersey meant more to him just now.

It had not been handed in.

'I hope you are thoroughly ashamed of yourself! Apologize to the driver! Apologize to the other children! A useless trip, a wasted morning—and all your fault! We would much rather have studied Bembridge. How old is the windmill there, someone?'

No one wanted to guess. He wasn't popular.

'Two hundred and twenty-five years, and it's made of wood. See what you've missed due to Nigel's stupidity! Now, this afternoon, to make up for lost time, instead of building sand-castles on the beach, you'll be exploring the camp and drawing a map of what you find. You will RV outside my chalet door for briefing at fourteen hundred hours exactly. And when I say "exactly", I mean "exactly"!'

They didn't care whether he meant it or not.

At lunch, the Manager placed himself grimly by the service hatch to observe their misdemeanours. The ache in Miss Hodge's ankle moved to her head. She babbled helplessly to Mr Bluett:

'Mixed football this afternoon to restore morale, don't you think?'

'Football! Are you mad?'

'I simply thought . . .'

'You didn't think!'

'I'm not a mind-reader. As Miss Walsh has typed no programme . . .'

He listed his intentions: map-making this afternoon; church and ramble tomorrow; visits during the rest of the week to Osborne House, Carisbrooke Castle, Newtown Nature Reserve and Godshill Village; a boat trip at Yarmouth; a trek over Tennyson Down from Farringford to Alum Bay; diary and letter periods; field studies; rock climbing; evening cricket; last night bonfire . . .

In principle it sounded excellent.

The Manager bustled over. He had removed his spectacles and was rubbing the lenses with his handkerchief.

'Some of your children are pouring HP Sauce into the water jugs. The black boy has just called the waitress a four letter word!'

'The "black boy", as you call our young negro friend, is no worse than the rest.'

'Allow me to finish, sir, if you please! The state of the chalets this morning! The maids tell me . . .'

'I don't think we need worry Miss Hodge with minor details.'

'One chalet only appeared to be in the same condition as when your school arrived. Chalet No 26. A single child.'

'And the child?' Mr Bluett smiled with sarcastic self-satisfaction. 'None other than the black boy you've been complaining of!'

Miss Hodge touched the Manager's arm.

'I'll come to your office afterwards.'

The Manager deferred. It was as though an unspoken message had passed between them. Damn Muriel anyhow! What business was it of hers! If she lent a hand with manners, calling the roll, and issuing pocket money and late night cake and milk! *That* he would appreciate! Not only was she not assisting him this summer, she was muddying the water! Next she'd be choosing what best to see and do upon the island, when everything she knew about it she had learned from him! Wasn't it she who on their first School Journey asked, 'Does a North wind blow from the North or towards it?' Now she was headmistress she couldn't keep her place . . .

F*   169

'Was it right, do you think, to put Nigel in a chalet by himself?'

'There was one place over, Muriel. We're not an even number.'

'Yes, but of all the children who should not feel isolated . . .'

Muriel was telling *him*—the only member of staff who gave his undivided attention to the boy, who considered his welfare more earnestly perhaps than did his own mother!

'I think I can claim to understand his needs better than you do!'

'You would grant me the right, though, to express an opinion? Doesn't what you've done suggest a form of segregation?'

'I will not have the boy corrupted.'

'Really, Francis! You must be thinking of those boarding schools you went to!'

'Because of his colour he'd be blamed for. . . . Do you mind if I forego the cheese? I have to prepare this afternoon's equipment.'

'Francis, you're tired. Can I help in any way at all?'

'No, you can not.'

Disposed towards efficiency, he appeared at his chalet door at fourteen hundred hours. Only three out of twenty-five children had arrived.

'They'll get a hundred lines apiece for every time I blow the whistle!'

Gary, the last of them, reported after three quarters of an hour.

'Hands out of pockets! Where have you been?'

'Watching a pheasant's nest in the nettles.'

He'd been playing with a football on the beach.

'You knew the RV! No free half-hour tonight! See me for lines in the ballroom! The same goes for the other twenty-one. And now to the business in hand! Each one of you is to make a map of Greygates. I will submit the best for inclusion in the Management's brochure next year. I told some of you last night how to read a compass, and your first main task will be to measure direction and take a compass bearing. You will work in groups. Lorraine will lead one, Gary another, Nigel another . . . Leaders will remember that their compasses indicate the magnetic north. A magnetic bearing is the angle between the magnetic north and the object being observed, reading in a clockwise direction. For instance, the oak tree over there has a bearing of . . .'

The needle wouldn't remain steady.

'Oh well, let's say it's about two hundred and sixteen degrees. By the way, to make it more interesting for the cricketers amongst us, we will measure in chains. I've cut five lengths of rope, each half a chain. There are ten chains in a furlong, and eight furlongs in a mile. Yes, Gary! You've a question?'

'Wouldn't it be better to work in metres?'

'I can't think why!'

'The Common Market, sir.'

'To hell with the Common Market!'

'Sorry, sir!'

'It is now fourteen fifty-eight hours. Set your watches. I shall move amongst you, but leaders will keep in touch with me every fifteen minutes. Should anything go wrong, wave a white handkerchief. Fall out, collect your equipment, and proceed!'

Nigel said he didn't want to be the leader of a chain-gang.

'Less of the clever-clever, Nigel, and get cracking!'

Sleeplessness. Doors slamming. The tinny clash of bins and trays in distant kitchens.

In bush hat, anorak and corduroy, Mr Bluett was about the camp by seven, hoping a boy or girl, but best of all his Nigel, would peep from a chalet window and ask for a game of tennis or an early morning swim. Instead, he would find dog-eared comics splayed lifeless on the chairs and shrubbery, with his rain-gauge and thermometer thrown or kicked among the dew-soaked verges, and the wreckage of a paper dart protruding from a gutter. There was silence everywhere—a coherent pact to oust and to ignore him. The gardeners, even—cutting, hoeing, raking, planting in preparation for the season—failed to acknowledge his hello. The milkman and the baker drove away at his approach. Thrushes, scouting for worms, flew into the trees. The dalmatian never bounded, the pony never trotted, to his side. Nothing, no one seemed to want him, despite his exertions from dawn till nightfall when drunkenly he crashed into the chalets on his rounds, and children held their breaths and hid quite still beneath the bedclothes for fear of his touching or addressing them.

171

On several outings, a hobbling Muriel attempted to take charge. Was it a figment of his alcoholic nightmare? He would not have been more astounded if a bird of night had sat, even at noonday, upon a tower of Carisbrooke Castle.

Mr Lacey moved among the children of Adelaide Bing at mealtimes with meddling effrontery. 'Hand me that knife you pocketed! A fork is a comb?'

'I wonder, Lacey, if in the mornings you'd play your transistor a shade less loudly. My children are here to savour the sounds of the countryside.'

'Permission to submit a more urgent protest? A boy of mine is missing a yellow shirt! One of your boys has stolen it.'

'Not one of your own, needless to say!'

'Not one of mine.'

'Wendale Manor during its tempestuous history has harboured not a single thief?'

'Wendale Manor during its distinguished history has neither harboured a thief nor anyone black, and a black thief was seen leaving one of our chalets bearing a yellow shirt.'

'I take exception to your crediting an idle tale. I shall prove beyond doubt that you are in the wrong. When is this supposed to have happened?'

'Before supper.'

'Very well. Tonight I shall inspect Nigel's chest of drawers and suitcase. Will that satisfy you? Will you accept my word when I tell you I found nothing?'

'*If* you tell me you found nothing!'

'Mr Lacey, if Nigel has stolen this yellow shirt, my head-mistress, I assure you, will be informed immediately and the garment restored to you with fullest apologies. Meanwhile if you would be good enough to control your radio . . .'

He staggered from the bar at closing time. The floodlit fountain spumed in the centre of its artificial lake. On the sea beyond the cliffs, a cabin-cruiser glittered Francewards. Bats flitted low around the strings of chalets clustered back to back amid converging meadows. A rabbit hopped near the alley-lamp by whose glare Mr Bluett now endeavoured to insert a key into Nigel's lock.

He risked the light-switch. Nigel lay motionless beneath a mound of bedclothes. Mr Bluett opened every drawer and riffled

172

through its contents. Here were two flintstones! Here a giant whelk and, marked in biro and miss-spelt, a 'Cuttel Fish for Binkie Budgie'! No tipsy father returning late to kith and kin and wandering a nursery to glimpse his child in artless slumber, to kiss its brow and touch in tenderness its most cherished toys and baubles, could have felt more proud and loving.

Gently he slid Nigel's suitcase from underneath the bed-bunk to the middle of the floor. He raised the lid.

'Nigel! *Nigel!* Wake up and explain yourself!'

Aghast, an unhappy Jason, he stood above his discovery—a yellow shirt in which nestled ashtrays, paper weights, a Toby jug, key-rings, bottle-openers, butter-knives and caddy-spoons, all stolen from the Greygates shop.

'Nigel! This shirt! And what about the rest? Bought with the twenty pennies I've issued you each day? I'm speaking to you, Nigel!'

He ripped the sheets and blankets off the bed. Nigel lay naked there. Lorraine was in his arms.

'Desdemona! Return to your chalet. This instant!'

A flurrie of nightie, a scampering, the thud of a distant door, and it was possible, for Nigel's sake, to forget the wrong that she had done.

'Quickly, Nigel! Get your clothes on!'

Nigel obeyed. Was it due to fear of the consequences of refusal, Mr Bluett asked himself, or the full realization that his teacher was his friend and wished to help him?

'You're shivering! Don't worry! Trust me! I've told you before—I'm on your side! Wait here!'

He fetched a torch.

'Ready? Good! Close your suitcase. That's right. Now give it to me. Come on. Quietly!'

Mr Lacey, returning from his own rounds, watched them cross to the stairs which led to the shore. He ran to warn Muriel in her chalet. Both of them hurried to the edge of the cliffs.

Walking hand in hand in the moonlight upon a cape of rocks were the two figures, one tall, one small, the former with a suit-case. They were like two renegades escaping—but from what, to where, and how and why?

Mr Bluett put the suitcase down and opened it.

'Take these ashtrays first! Throw them as far out as you

can! The exercise should improve your bowling! When did you steal them, Nigel?' He threw the Toby jug. 'If I'm to continue helping'—splash—'you'll have to tell me!'

'After meals, you and Miss Hodge usually stay talking . . . I'm not the only one!'

'I'm not interested in the others! You put your hand under the grid?'

'There's a window at the back. We hoist one another up.'

Key-rings, bottle-openers, butter-knives, caddy-spoons—in turn they had submerged. Nigel took out the shirt. It flapped its signal to the couple watching from above.

'By jingo!' nudged Mr Lacey. 'Our missing garment! Look! They're burying it in the sand!'

'The cost—how much do I owe you? Take me back, please, to my chalet!'

While she was brewing Mr Lacey tea on her solid fuel burner, Mr Bluett was tucking Nigel up in bed.

'Goodnight!' He kissed him lightly on the cheek.

No response.

'I said "Goodnight!"!'

'Goodnight!'

When the door was shut, Nigel ran to the basin and washed his face clean. He had almost grown to like Boozy-Woozy-Pickled-Gherkin-Brandy-Blottoguts, and now he hated him again. He was a queer.

4

'A gentleman is someone who knows the conventions of society. A gentleman is never unintentionally rude. A gentleman is always courteous and kind. A gentleman is accustomed to lead. A gentleman is someone to whom the lower orders instinctively say "sir". You, Nigel, are now a young gentleman. Goodbye and good luck to you!' . . .

With so much to achieve before seeing Nigel off the premises, Mr Bluett resented Lady Sandra's Nature periods more than ever.

'There's a slow-worm in my potting shed. He's a kind of lizard without legs, and he freezes when he sees you. He's lost his tail, but there's a neat little conical stump where a new one will grow!'

At such an important juncture of Nigel's career, wouldn't she be better teaching him to recite:

'Our England is a garden, and such gardens are not made
By singing: "Oh, how beautiful!" and sitting in the
shade . . .'?

'At last the roses in my garden are shouting "Summer!"' she announced in the staff-room.

'You don't say!' mocked Colin.

'Unfortunately, Pussy has hurt my clematis while trying to kill a goldcrest.'

Mr Bluett challenged her.

'A goldcrest in your clematis?'

A finch or a sparrow in her clematis, yes! A goldcrest, never! That was it! Her Blackheath garden was a fancy, a myth created for the benefit of Adelaide Bing!

'Yes, Mr Bluett. An orange and tangerine crest. Feathers olive and green, shading to light lime. You must have seen one. Or maybe you have and didn't realize it. Their bodies are so tiny, they can be taken for sunbeams shimmering through the leaves.'

Mr Bluett roses to his feet and glowered down at her.

'To be honest, Lady Sandra, your clematis and your goldcrest bore the pants off me!'

Lizzie sprang to her defence.

'No more, I'm sure, than your Commonwealth bores the pants off Lady Sandra!'

'How dare you speak for Lady Sandra! You're not fit to polish her shoes!'

He stalked from the room.

'The climacteric!' laughed Lizzie.

'Booze!' laughed Colin.

'Ni—' began Lady Sandra. 'Nigel!' they laughed together.

Nigel came to nets because his mother made him. He practised the high jump, the long jump and the hundred yards because he wanted to. Whatever the reasons, Mr Bluett was encouraged. He might take the boy to Edinburgh to watch the Commonwealth Games. And, had the match against St Bridget's not clashed with the Test between England and Pakistan, they could have spent the next Saturday at Lord's again.

Nigel was given time off, and money, to buy a cap that fitted him, and for three whole days, while non-team ran amok, a commandeered eleven were shown how to bowl full tosses and leg-cutters, how to make a block, how to hook a pull and how to drive the ball between cover and mid-off. 'Catches win matches' they were told. 'Quick changes between overs buy time in which to attack the enemy'. They did not listen. They did not understand. They stiffly ambled this way and that, exaggerating their efforts to grow accustomed to wearing pads and treating these intensive preparations as a delectable farce.

On Friday afternoon, the definitive Team was posted, and at twenty-four minutes past eight on Saturday morning, Mr Bluett arrived at Front Gate, twenty-one minutes in advance of when those listed had been instructed to join him.

He was obliged to wait till eight-thirty before ringing the Fuehrer's bell to gain admission. Though, with the exception of Muriel, he was the longest serving member of staff, he had never been allocated a key. It angered him that the youthful Coote could have one. The injustice blemished this blue June day. So did having to field a team not dressed in white. He had never learned to accept St Bridget's collective expression of disdain at the approach of his own boisterous motley. 'Our turn-out doesn't compare favourably.' He had made the point to Muriel again and again. She remained apathetic.

A woman in cerise—hat, handbag, shoes, lipstick—wafted past him. A bookie's mistress? A parent he should have raised his hat to?

The schoolkeeper opened the door.

'Not ring punctual on a St Bridget's day, Mr Bluett! I came to see if the bell was out of order!'

Had it been cowardice to join with the rest in reviling the Fuehrer? Wasn't he reliable, loyal and efficient—a man after his own heart?

'Thank you. A moment's reverie.'

He awaited the children in his classroom. Nigel and Gary must control the bowling. Fielders must remember not to shout 'How's 'at!' from every position in the event of LBW's. Last year, deep square leg appealed, and displeased an umpire.

He re-checked the kit. Bats. Gloves. Muriel should have agreed to replace the shrivelled right-hand ones three years ago! Nigel's cap. Pads. Left put with left again! . . .

Eight forty-three. The team were due at eight forty-five. They cut things as fine as this because they lived so close. Some, he supposed, must wait for the Fuehrer to ring the bell in the mornings before jumping out of bed. Today, though, Nigel had promised to come early so as to learn when to alter the placing of the field.

Eight forty-five. He verified the notice: A Match Will Be Played On Saturday 19th Against St Bridget's At Parliament Hill Fields. Wickets Will Be Pitched At 10.00 A.M. Team And Scorer Report To Classroom 1B At 8.45 A.M. Bus Fares: 16P Return.'

His watch must be fast. No, the reverse—the electric clock on the wall read eight forty-seven! What the deuce was happening? After the practice yesterday, he had urged upon each of them the need for punctuality.

He unpinned the notice and clipped it to a scoring book he

took from his desk drawer. He put the book in the kit bag, which he carried, with a couple of extra bats, to the top of the stairs. There he rested to take a swig of brandy before grunting and puffing with his load down to the street.

Where could those confounded blighters be? Shading his eyes, he peered into the distance. A child was sauntering in his direction. He waited for the face to clarify, but it belonged to no one that he knew.

The door of the Lodge was open. He knocked at it.

'Who's there?'

'Bluett!'

'Come inside!'

Staff rarely received a 'Come inside!' from the Fuehrer. His home was an Eagle's Nest, a Berchtesgaden from which even the Lady Sandra was once expelled when she ventured there to borrow a pan for making mint and apple jelly.

'Very kind of you . . . Just wondering if you happen to have seen any of my cricketers.'

The Fuehrer was holding a spanner in the dim interior.

'I said, "Come in!" I'm fixing a pipe. There'll be a flood if I leave it any longer.'

'No, thanks. I just hope that Nigel . . . the Captain at least . . . Did anyone ring?'

'No one.'

'The clocks are right?'

'You go back and watch awhile. The missus will bring you out a cup of strong black coffee.'

Ever since School Journey he'd heard the parents chattering at the gate. Should they, shouldn't they withdraw their children? Was it safe to leave them in Mr Bluett's custody? Miss Hodge knew, *he* knew, everyone except Mr Bluett knew that the fixture against St Bridget's had been discreetly cancelled. But it was Miss Hodge's place, not a schoolkeeper's, to inform Mr Bluett of the facts.

Mr Bluett returned.

'No sign . . . There must be some misunderstanding. Thanks for your help.'

'Your cup of coffee!'

'I'm sorry, but by the time I've taken the equipment back to my classroom . . .'

178

'I'll do that.'

He had never known the Fuehrer to assist. Who would have guessed such kindness lurked beneath that gruff façade!

'Thank you. That really is most sporting. I must get to Parliament Hill Fields as soon as possible. St Bridget's will be almost there. They've got to be informed.'

'Take my advice! Don't fret yourself! Have your coffee first!'

'*Someone* has to fret round here! I hardly expected you, of all men, to show such irresponsibility!'

At Parliament Hill Fields, an elkhound and a setter frisked upon the pitch in mutually conducive states of micturition. Around the boundaries roamed elderly men with sticks, and boys on bicycles. There was no sign of St Bridget's or of Adelaide Bing, yet Mr Bluett still conjured with the notion of an abject Captain's panting arrival to explain the mix-up.

Half an hour elapsed. Mr Bluett's flask was empty. It was not yet opening time. To ease the shock of the morning's events, he bought more Hennessy at the nearest off-licence. Then, after telephoning St Bridget's from a call-box and getting no reply, he hailed a taxi to Magnolia Court.

Harry answered his impatient rings and rattles.

'What the . . .!!'

'May I speak to Nigel!'

'No, you may not!'

'He and the school cricket team were to meet me at eight forty-five!'

'Nigel isn't in.'

'His mother, then.'

'She ain't in neither. Now buzz off! Why not speak to your bloody headmistress. It were 'er, weren't it, who told them not to bloody come?'

'Nonsense!'

'Want this fist, mate, bang in the middle of your mush?'

'Why this attitude? I am only doing my best for Nigel!'

'Give over!!'

Harry slammed the door.

An angry and unsteady Mr Bluett reached Miss Hodge in Hackney by mid-afternoon.

'Francis!'

She supported him up the narrow staircase that led to her one spare room.

'You've creased it!'

He had fallen on the bedspread. He let her push and shift and re-arrange him so as to remove it and lay it safely folded on a chair. 'Against so petty a female', he thought, 'my aspirations never stood a chance!'

Without daring to loosen his collar and tie, she crept away.

'Come along now! Tea-time! Up we get!' she called an hour later. ' "Come along!" I said! Tea-time! Tea-time! Up we get!'

The uninvolved, headmistressy voice, the voice that had haunted work and leisure for so many fruitless years, intensified the painful thudding in Mr Bluett's skull. She might have been speaking to a child resting in the medical room after a nose-bleed, and not to a colleague who understood her every whim and weakness, and who used to help her hold her aitches and mind her p's and q's.

'Yes, yes, Muriel! Coming! Coming down to tea!'

Clothes crumpled, glazed of eye, he dragged himself to her table.

'How many lumps? I forget.'

'Two.'

'One, two—there we are! And three slices of barm-brack. Excuse fingers!'

'I don't want any barm-brack, and I don't much feel like drinking this tea.'

'Don't be petulant, Francis! It's better for you than tippling from that flask of yours!'

'Answer me! Did you or did you not cancel the St Bridget's match behind my back?'

She gathered her cardigan about her and picked at crumbs upon her plate.

'I was asked to do so by several parents.'

'The children knew?'

'Yes.'

'Including Nigel?'

'I sent him to you with the message.'

'I shall expect an apology from him in Assembly!'

'No, Francis! This is where you've to drop all interest in Nigel whatever. I want you to grant him his freedom.'

'Freedom?'

'Forget him! Leave him be! Put him right out of your mind!'

The winsome probationer, the ingénue in flimsy silk, with wide revers and flouncing skirts, was now advising *him*, and expecting him to kow-tow! How this room had changed since her unpretentious mother had died there, and Muriel, a neither Yes nor No, had climbed to a higher branch of the educational bonsai tree! What a shallow nobody she was! She had failed herself as well as him. Was it her idea of progress to replace the old black-leaded grate by an electric one, topped with red lumps of illuminated glass; the rag rugs and parquet-patterned lino by a fitted woollen carpet; bunches of Honesty and Everlastings by peacocks' feathers and large paper roses from Harrods; a plush-draped softwood table by the naked slippery utensil of walnut veneer at which they were now seated?!

'And if I considered it my duty not to obey?'

'So much the worse for you! Your goodwill is beginning to appear indelicate.'

'Indelicate?'

Hadn't she already resolved to dismiss him? Why, she asked herself, bother to explain? It would make no difference whether he agreed with her or not.

'I wish to hear no more about you and Nigel. Believe me, he isn't worth it.'

'In whose opinion?'

'We are all God's creatures. Nigel is worth no more attention than the rest. Francis, I have never known you to appear so *unmanly*!'

'Meaning?'

'You have allowed an unexceptional little boy of eleven to get the better of you. A drink is a drink . . . What I mean is, in the past your drinking did not appear to affect your work. Now, your work, namely Nigel, appears to be affecting your drinking!'

'If I drink more than I ought, Muriel—and, in my view, I drink less than I must—it's because of you, Muriel, and not because of Nigel. You remain in your "power-house" quite unscathed, while I have to shoulder the problems of Adelaide Bing, single-handed!'

'A better man would call my dislike of interfering my strength. Well, I am interfering now, Francis. You consider it "shouldering problems" to conceal Nigel's thefts on School Journey?'

Mr Bluett, whose hand had shot to his breast pocket, was gawping at her in astonishment.

'Go on, Francis! Help yourself! You'll need it!'

She was tired, suddenly, of being tactful. She had let him play Prince Regent for too long.

'Theft? I don't think I follow.'

He swigged ostentatiously to hide the pretence.

'A buried yellow shirt. Other objects entrusted to Davy Jones's locker.'

'Sorry! You are addressing a man who is entirely baffled!'

'And you are addressing a woman who knows you are less baffled than you make out! Tell me, what lengths are you prepared to go to on behalf of this young villain, Francis? Have you thrown all reason to the winds?'

'What's the point of discussing it with you! You never help!'

'You in need of help from me, Francis! Come, come! You think the boot is on the other foot. This afternoon I have offered guidance, and you have complained bitterly!'

'You have held a bullet to my back. You have ordered me to renounce all interest in my boy!'

'*Your* boy! Careful! Careful!'

'*My* boy! He has no one else!'

'He has his mother!' . . .

So meandered their conversation, while they hardened in their views—Mr Bluett that Nigel was his hundredth sheep, Miss Hodge that Mr Bluett was no longer hers.

'Till Monday, then, Francis! And, let me repeat that, for his remaining five weeks with us, Nigel is to be mine, not yours—mine and everybody else's. I shall expect you to take an interest in *every* member of your class. What is more, I shall expect to see a Scheme of Work. Choose a topic.'

'Really, Muriel! You don't have to tell your grandfather how to suck eggs! For the whole of the spring I did the Commonwealth!'

'So I gather! Why not do the Isle of Wight? Talk with, not at, the children for a change! Make Lesson Plans which allow for the girls' and boys' intuitive and emotional needs! We are living in two civilizations concurrently, Francis—the old one of the brain and the new one of the senses. Knowledge, obedience, loyalty, public spirit, duty and self-sacrifice lead to non-involvement. Experience and awareness lead to socialism.'

'I can only surmise that you heard this balderdash at the last Headteachers' Conference!'

She ushered him to the hall door, and, in the days that followed, nobody divined from his demeanour in the classroom, nor from hers as she lazed in traditional isolation behind her study desk, that this discomfiting encounter had taken place.

'Hands up the cricket team! Why was I not informed that St Bridget's were so ill-mannered as to postpone our fixture? Well I intend to punish all concerned. There shall be no match between you and St Bridget's this season, and no more cricket whatever for yourselves! Nigel, as Captain and chief offender in bringing me unnecessarily from home on Saturday, you will write me out two hundred times: "There can be no stable and balanced development of the mind, apart from the assumption of responsibility"!'

Retribution exacted and honour satisfied, charity was again extended, and he prepared Nigel (a natural athlete in no need of training) for Sports Day, and rehearsed a class reading from 'Uncle Tom's Cabin' for the Summer Concert, with Nigel in the title rôle.

Why were teachers afraid to proselytize, evangelize and be didactic?! The more he watched the other members of staff in the throes of their own end-of-term preparations—Lady Sandra sewing muslin masks for a 'Beatrix Potter Pageant', and Colin and Lizzie vertically co-operating in a 'Percussion Musical' with sticks and jam jars—the more he believed that wherever art makes itself felt, truth seems to be absent. When, on July the seventh, the Government announced that the security and prosperity of the United Kingdom would best be served by British accession to the European Communities, he flaunted his flask shamelessly before the children, shouting, 'England is a sceptred Isle no longer!'

He was very drunk when Muriel, true to her word, called to examine his Scheme of Work and the Lesson Plans he had failed to furnish. To the exclusion of the fidgety remainder of the class, his intoxicated faculties were concentrated on the truculent Nigel precisely as she had forbidden.

' ". . . When we can love and pray over all and through all, the battle's past and the victory's come—glory be to God!" And, with streaming eyes and choking voice, the black man looked up to heaven . . .'

'Nigel, interpret! What does Mrs Stowe intend us, and you above all, to learn from this passage?'

Miss Hodge could scarcely control her irritation.

'May I see your Lesson Plans, Mr Bluett? This is Religious Instruction, I presume. Your topic?'

'The Common Market,' he extemporized.

'The Common Market! Isn't the connection between "Uncle Tom's Cabin" and the Common Market somewhat tenuous? Your structuring, in my opinion, leaves a lot to be desired!'

'Quite come out of our little cage, haven't we, Muriel?!' The children were agog. 'Fortunately I have studied the Treaty of Rome with greater attention than you, my dear. If we enter Europe, Nigel, our negro friend here'—he swayed as he spoke—'is likely to be downgraded from a second- to a third-class citizen. He'll be needing all the inspiration he can get from the likes of Mrs Stowe! So shall we all! We shall all be slaves of a Business Consortium in Brussels!'

'Tripe and onions!'

She swept from the room.

'Let us continue! . . . "And this, O Africa! latest called of nations—called to the crown of thorns, the scourge, the bloody sweat, the cross of agony—this is to be *thy* victory; by this shalt thou reign with Christ when His kingdom shall come on earth."—What, Nigel, do you say to *that*?'

'Up the Gunners!'

'And I say that *that* will cost you another two hundred lines! Come and see me at break!'

Were his colleagues correct? Was there no exalted thing in the whole of God's creation towards which Nigel could respond with dignity?

Luckily, a moment later, Mr Bluett saw the boy in a shaft of sunlight with dust-specks dancing round his curly, chiselled head, and it was plain to him again that Nigel was the centre of the

184

universe and that something, one day, would elicit from him a noble action worthy of his teacher's labours.

Sports Day. Despite a moment's anxiety before the first event, when a grinning Nigel was to be seen, grass in hair and skipping up and down and waving a length of rope, the occasion seemed to vindicate Mr Bluett's confidence, and compensate for all the ignominies he had suffered in the name of the Black Commonwealth. From the Whip Pen he could meet the eye of his adversaries unflinchingly while they carried out the tasks it was his lot, as organizer, to set them—The Fuehrer as Starter, Lady Sandra and Colin Coote as Placing Judges, Miss Walsh as Recorder, and Lizzie Oates as Spectator Supervisor.

Nigel was winner of Boys' Top Year Field events, having cleared three foot six inches in the High Jump and eleven foot three inches in the Long. He now limbered beside the track, his coach willing him to appal Hitler and his quislings with his prowess, as did Jesse Owen at Munich in the Olympian year of 1936.

Mr Bluett spoke through his loud hailer:

'Will boys of the Top Year please take position for the Bean Bag Race. I will repeat that. Will boys of the Top Year please take position for The Bean Bag Race. Only five entrants have reported to me and there should be twelve.'

Lizzie Oates was letting competitors go to the public drinking fountains as usual.

'Very well! Let the race start without them!' Nigel would have beaten the others anyhow!

'. . . Go!' shouted the Fuehrer in his brown overall.

What a figure of a boy! What a relaxed style! Look at those pectorals, visible even through his vest! No, no! Never risk throwing the bags into the buckets! . . . Yes! In with the last one! Take up thy bucket and *run*! Run, man, run! Give it all you've got! . . . Bravo! Let your detractors fault you now if they can! High Jump, Long Jump, Bean Bag Race! . . . Loosen up! That's right! Breathe deeply before the Spud and Spoon!

'On your marks! Get set! Go!'

Mr Bluett left the Whip Pen, and ran beside the entrants to ensure fair play.

'Swing your hips, Nigel! Swing your hips! . . . Gary, you're

185

disqualified! Sorry, no protesting! You kicked it forward when you dropped it! Yes you did—a good two yards! . . . Hey! I saw you push!'

Like a sniper, he picked off challengers. He did not perceive that Nigel, the winner by an easy margin, kept his potato in position with a wadge of chewing-gum.

'Miss Oates! Take the names, please, of those children who booed!'

'It was a group of parents.'

'Would you believe it! Booing a little boy because of his pigmentation!'

'They were booing you!'

'Sorry, haven't time to discuss . . . The top year girls have to be marshalled.'

Before the Relay, whose conclusion, in the absence of Miss Hodge, signalled the majority of children to dash into the busy streets unsupervised, came the Hundred Yards.

At last must Caucasoid and Mongoloid capitulate, concede inferiority! Every person present—participator, spectator, man, woman, boy, girl—must admit to Nigel's supreme agility, the synergy of his co-ordination, the pre-eminent beauty of a mind relating to each ligament and muscle! Legs loose, back flat; elbows swinging to the side at ninety degrees; fingers curled and pointing upwards—textbook stuff maybe, but transmuted by this schoolchild into a poetry of flexion and extension neither Wyomia Tyus nor Robert Lee Hayes could have rivalled in their acme!

With what pride in the past and hope for the future Mr Bluett travelled to Adelaide Bing the following morning! He did not remonstrate against the jostling on the Earl's Court platforms. To touch or be touched was to share the felicity of being. He bade the ticket-collector good morning at his destination.

Miss Hodge was already ensconced behind her desk under Picasso's 'Young Man and Horse', one of many regulation reproductions she had dotted through the building.

'Morning, Muriel! Nigel fairly romped home yesterday! Three foot six in the High Jump. Eleven foot three in the Long. I can't tell you how many miles per hour he went at in the Hundred Yards! By comparison, the other boys looked tame . . . !'

186

'Sit yourself down, Francis. I warn you, this won't be pleasant news . . .'

For a frightening second he thought Nigel had been killed in some accident. He said :

'Come out with it, Muriel! If you want me to take a lower class next year, say so!'

'I've been asked to let you go.'

'Go where?'

'The Managers have asked me to suspend you.'

'Suspend me from what?'

'You've been fired, Francis!'

He sat non-plussed. Though his mouth was droughty, his clothes clung to him like an armour-plate of ice. 'Fired'. She had blurted out the word as if it were the last contraction of a woman in labour who has found the pain of it worthwhile. This aimless creature who, in times gone by and when it suited her, made no secret of her dependence on his counsel, and who, as the years advanced, when given responsibility, was no more capable of leadership than his female batman would have been in the front line, had now dismissed him!

'You are not yourself, Muriel. Muriel never makes decisions.'

'Reverse this one if you can!'

'Heartiest congratulations! So you're sending the old war-horse out to graze now that it has served its purpose! I understand the drill!'

'Francis, I pity you!'

He rose from his seat. His arms hung limply. His shoulders sagged.

She leaned across to him. 'It's not the end of the world. What about a private school?'

'And my beliefs? What about equality in England's green and pleasant land?'

'Cricket, Latin, "God save the Queen", stiff upper lip . . . A prep school, Francis, would fit you like a glove!'

'And what is to happen to the Nigels?'

'All right then! The African states recruit teachers every year. Misfits have been known to land on their own feet . . .'

He could bear no more. His hand yanked convulsively at the door-knob. His back was shuddering.

187

'Oh, just one other thing! Drop that "Uncle Tom's Cabin" business you're preparing for the concert!'

'But Nigel has the main part!'

'I said "Drop it!"'

He rounded on her.

'And I suppose he's to get no prize on Prize Day!'

'I can think of no one in the school less suitable.'

'Sportsman of the Year?'

'No, Francis!'

She looked at her watch.

'Bigot!'

She ignored him and began to talc her nose.

Lady Sandra was embroidering Tabitha Twitchit's eyebrows. Miss Oates was testing batteries. Mr Coote was twanging a harp he'd made with rubber bands.

'I've been given the push!' The trio, like a jury which had found him guilty, spared him not a glance. 'I've been asked to resign!'

'On what grounds?'

Lady Sandra bent, as she spoke, in search of a different coloured thread.

'Can't you guess?'

'And there's to be a salary increase!' wailed Coote evasively.

'Want a cup of slosh?'

Now, when the damage to which she had contributed was irreparable, the brash youngster who had complained that to 'tutor' Nigel was against Union rules, manifested a disposition to unbend! To accept tea from her hands would be to steal a comforting kiss from the lips of a distempered harlot.

'I'll pour my own.'

Coote and Oates croaked jestingly when he added brandy. Lady Sandra lost poise:

'The man is not a laughing matter. He has brought disgrace upon us all!'

'Please explain!' thundered Mr Bluett.

'That boy you protect! Your criticism of the ways we've tried to handle him! Your alcoholic . . .'

Miss Oates again perversely rallied to Mr Bluett's defence:

'I sympathize with Africa Unbound—'

'Mr Bluett binds Nigel hand and foot!' interrupted Colin.

'Exactly!' cried Lady Sandra. 'Our Mr Bluett is a fraud!'

They were speaking amongst themselves as if he wasn't there. He listened with resentment and disgust, then shouted:

'The three of you, with the concurrence of Miss Hodge, have victimized Nigel, and, with the assistance of the Managers, ruined *me*!'

'Cobblers!'

Miss Oates impatiently gathered up her batteries and left the room with Coote flapping close at heel.

'Such lovely manners! "Cobblers"! An inspired choice of watchword for Women's Liberation!'

Lady Sandra stuffed her bits and pieces into her basket and, sailing towards the door, delivered this farewell rebuke:

'I speak not only as a woman, not only as a teacher, but as a mother too. I am glad that you are leaving us! You are beneath contempt.'

He retched into the lavatory sink, then braced himself once more with brandy. Was he fated never to know justice on this earth? An accusation of that kind from Lady Sandra!—Lady Sandra who would tiptoe so as not to harm the earwigs on her garden paths!

Nigel headed the queue already formed to pay Gary the Dinner Money. The classroom swirled. The floor rocked.

He crumpled down into his chair.

Children were frightened.

'OK?'

'Need an Alkaseltser?'

'Want me to get Miss 'Odge?'

He was moved by their concern. They watched bemused as bead after bead formed at the tip of his nose and fell in ever quickening succession—splat, splat, splat—onto the cover of his register.

'I've done the Dinner Money, Sir!'

'Thank you, Gary. Bring it to me, will you?'

'Cheer up, sir!'

Gary's whispered exhortation increased his melancholy. Why couldn't this concern be Nigel's!

A girl, whom for three terms he had ignored, now anxiously helped Gary take control:

189

'Want us to line them up for Assembly?'

'Please do that . . .' Mr Bluett searched his mind for her name. Nigel, Nigel, Nigel, was all that he could find. 'I'll be marking in the staff-room should anyone inquire. Lead on!'

All the children filed out sensibly—save for Nigel. Only Nigel misbehaved. Only Nigel shouted on the stairs.

A feeling of resentment mounted inside Mr Bluett. 'I have heard of black boys, Nigel's age,' he thought, 'who have gratefully toiled twenty miles a day in order to write their lessons on a slate! Yet Nigel, for whom every luxury is provided, cannot, in part-payment, reach Assembly without creating a disturbance!'

He unfastened a map of Africa on the wall, folded it, and took it to a cupboard in the corner. He crouched to put it on one of the lower shelves.

He heard chinking. Someone was at his desk. Miss Walsh already hounding him for Dinner Money! He stood to chide her:

'Oh ye of little faith!'

Nigel's fingers were as if spellbound in the Dinner Box.

'Miss Hodge sent me back to find my hymn book!'

'But not to thieve!' Mr Bluett had reached the boy through seven rows of desks, and was shaking him. 'Not . . . to . . . tell . . . lies . . .!'

'Lemme go, white pig! White boozy bastard!'

'You abuse your only friend!' He banged Nigel's face against the blackboard. 'You abuse your Master . . .! Eeenie, Meenie, Mainee, Mo! Catch a nigger by the toe. If he hollers let him go! . . .' Now he was hitting Nigel with a ruler and kicking, kicking, kicking him as though he were a football. 'Eenie, Meenie, Mainee, Mo! You—are—It!'